Dragon Wall: A Great Wall Novel

Millie Nelson Samuelson
Yesterday's Stories for Today's Inspiration

"I love *Dragon Wall*! I can't even express how much I enjoyed it, especially knowing it was about the author's family. Millie's parents endured so much for God. I am in awe of the determination, dignity and love they displayed throughout their lives. What an exceptional family!"
~ Melissa Rees, author's mystery writing buddy

I absolutely loved *Hungry River*, and *Dragon Wall* is equal to it since it's like a continuing story. I loved reading about the author's childhood (Abbie in the novel), although it made me so sad at times. Then I think of who the author is right now, and I realize that without our Creator allowing these things to happen to her and her family, their faith would not be the witness that it is. Thank you, my "white Chinese" friend, for sharing your family's story.
~ Linda Wells, author's good friend

"*Hungry River* was a phenomenal novel! I missed the characters as soon as I read the final page and closed the book. I can't wait to walk with them again as their adventures continue here in *Dragon Wall*."
~ Katie Rizer, Chesterton-Porter Rotary Club

Author Millie was born in Xian, China, where she spent her childhood amidst the horrifying devastations of Japan's attempt to seize China during World War II, followed by China's civil war. In 1950 she and her family escaped to Hong Kong. In 1951 they moved to Taiwan (Formosa back then). Her historical novels are inspired by her family's century of China and Taiwan experiences. In the novels, the "fictional" journaler and narrator Abbie is Millie.

Dragon Wall:

A Great Wall Novel

Book Two
Yangtze Dragon Trilogy

Millie Nelson Samuelson
Yesterday's Stories for Today's Inspiration

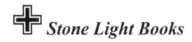
Stone Light Books

Dragon Wall:
A Great Wall Novel
Book Two
Yangtze Dragon Trilogy

Millie Nelson Samuelson
Yesterday's Stories for Today's Inspiration

Cover photo: A. Fred Nelson, pre-1950

millie@milliesbooks.org
www.milliesbooks.org
www.Amazon.com
(Kindle and paperback)

Published by: CreateSpace
ISBN: 978-1467913041

 **Stone Light Books**

for my wonderful parents
Fred and Blanche (Ivers) Nelson
whose China and Taiwan experiences
inspired this novel

and for my brother Doug
and our families
and our relatives
who share our heritage

and for all courageous multiculturalists
of faith like us
who sometimes adventure, sometimes suffer
to spread Light where there is darkness

Author's parents in 1936 in China. The novel's
"Alfred" and "Meggie" with "Donny."

*ten thousand fragrant thanks
to all the readers who have so graciously affirmed
my first novel, **Hungry River**,
and whose anticipation of **Dragon Wall**
has kept me joyfully motivated to finish*

*with special thanks to those who read
and commented on **Dragon Wall** as a manuscript
Doug Nelson, my brother
Beverly Beckon, my cousin
Linda Wells
Melissa Rees
Paul Brown*

*My family's true-life experiences inspired this novel. All of the
photos are from my father Fred Nelson's collection, most of them
taken by him pre-1950. Thanks, dear Dad!*
~ Millie Nelson Samuelson, 2012

Contents

Author's Introduction

If you can't wait to get to the novel, go on and read it, but be sure to come back and read this later. Promise?!

There I stood – the only "foreign devil" inside a high walled courtyard in Xian and surrounded by hundreds of Chinese.

Sixty years ago that situation would have alarmed me. Back then, Chairman Mao's Communists had just defeated General Chiang's Nationalists. And every time my American family ventured from home, angry crowds taunted us to get out of China. I remember once shouting back, "This IS my country! I was born here! Don't call me a foreign devil!" Mom quickly clamped her hand over my mouth and told me never to do that again.

I grew up hearing stories about rioting mobs brutally killing many of my missionary family's friends, both Chinese and Western, and even my father's fifteen year old sister. Although mobs frightened Mom and me, I never saw Dad afraid, not even sixty years ago when we precariously fled to Hong Kong and then Taiwan.

Fast forward through many decades to the amazing changes in China today. As the world's eyes increasingly focus on China, Westerners are now welcomed. Global headlines openly report dozens of new multi-millionaires and even billionaires in *Zhong Kuo*, the Central Kingdom, along with flood and earthquake devastations and human rights protests. Nor will the world soon forget China's spectacular hosting of the 2008 Olympics and the Chinese medal record, especially in gold.

And those hundreds of Chinese surrounding me earlier? We had not met before, but they greeted me warmly, then graciously ushered me to a worn wooden bench in their church's courtyard overflow. No, I was not afraid. Far from it, I was thrilled to be freely worshipping with devout Chinese Christians in Xian, the city of my birth. I was a witness to the crumbling of China's great wall against faith in God.

The church was registered with the government and therefore an official one. Several thousand men, women, and youth attended the services the morning I visited. Somewhat to my surprise, no one seemed concerned about openly carrying Bibles and chatting with me, an obvious American Christian. The worship was authentic and enthusiastic. I could understand enough of the minister's sermon to know her message was evangelical and inspiring.

Everyone attending church was well-dressed, except for the dozen or so beggars who lined the alleyway to the courtyard gate. That was about the only place I saw beggars during my most recent visit to China – a testimony to the generosity of Chinese Christians. As I gave to each beggar in Jesus' name, I remembered from my childhood the thousands of desperate, starving beggars who thronged the city streets and country roads, tragic victims of wars and famines.

Another person I gave to as I left church was a woman selling cross bracelets and necklaces she had made. With tears, she rapidly told me the many misfortunes concerning her only child. When I replied that I hadn't understood all her words, she was surprised.

"Oh, but you speak like a Chinese," she said. "I thought you could understand like one."

I explained about being born in Xian and spending my childhood there before my family went to Taiwan. I apologized for my poor understanding since I had not used Mandarin for many years. Then I asked her if she was a Christian.

"I am not yet a Christian," she answered.

"I will pray for you to become one soon. Then you will have God to help you with your problems," I encouraged her. I did not ask why she was not yet a believer. Everyone knows there are still reasons to fear becoming a Christian in China. One of her crosses hangs in my car, a constant reminder to pray for her and the church in China.

The following day I met another "not yet" Christian. At least, that's what the young man seemed like – or maybe he was one of China's secret Christians. He was our private tour guide when my husband Dave and I visited the site of the incredible terra cotta warriors.

As we viewed the thousands of larger-than-life clay soldiers, horses and chariots dating back to 200 B.C., we conversed more easily and personally with our guide than is possible in a larger group. He answered our questions in careful English. We found out he was a well-educated history teacher who had been unable to secure a teaching position. He told us his mother is a Christian who goes to church openly and regularly.

Although he didn't directly say so, sometimes in China relatives of Christians are punished. Was our guide a victim of that discriminatory practice?

* * *

I first met a Chinese secret Christian in America in the 1980s. Already an accomplished violinist, this young man had secured a coveted student visa to excel even more at one of our universities. On Sundays, he was visibly joyful at being able to worship aloud and freely. He shared with us about the secret worship services he had attended with his parents – services where they could only whisper, and where Communion was sometimes pretend juice and bread. At Christmas he asked us with a smile, "Can you imagine singing carols in a whisper?"

Now in the twenty-first century, millions of Chinese Christians are choosing to be secret no longer, regardless the consequences. More and more underground churches are giving up that status and growing rapidly as house churches. Sometimes they are raided and their members persecuted, but not nearly as often these days as formerly. State churches are thriving as well, such as the one I visited recently.

In 1950 when all Western missionaries had to leave China, including my family, it was estimated there were about three million Christians. Today in spite of decades of persecution, torture and untold numbers of deaths, the estimate according to some sources has soared to 120 million, which is approximately ten percent of China's 1.3 billion population. Even more exciting, Chinese Christians say it's their turn to be missionaries to the West where churches are dying and Christians have become complacent and lukewarm. Does that means we can look forward to a great world-wide revival? Many Christian leaders think so.

While it's true that Christians in China are still persecuted and sometimes detained or imprisoned without trials, such incidences are decreasing, especially in rapidly growing cities and urban areas. One reason is that many of China's newest Christians are wealthy and influential Party members. In fact, right now there may be as many Christians as Communist Party members. So it's no wonder that freedom of religion was clarified in China's constitution earlier this year, and that President Hu Jintao refers to modern China as a Socialist-Democracy.

*   *   *

PBS FRONTLINE/World aired a documentary on June 24, 2008, titled "Jesus in China." A three-page feature companion piece with the same title ran in *The Chicago Tribune* on the preceding Sunday, June 22, by the same correspondent and photographer, Evan Osnos and Jose M. Osorio.

"Chinese Christians believe this is their time to come out of the shadows," Osnos and Osorio reported. "These days Christians are getting bolder. The constitution [now] gives freedom of religion. China is experiencing a full-scale religious awakening [as] Christianity is slowly shedding the stigma of illegality."

Researchers Osnos and Osorio interviewed and photographed scores of Christians in China for the first time, and used many of their stories. These included Pastor Jin, who regularly pleads with his followers to attend only one service on Sundays so there will be room for the others waiting outside; business CEO and tycoon Mr. Zheng, who rides around in a chauffeured silver Rolls-Royce; economics Professor Zhao who became a Christian after studying the positive impact of Christianity on a country's economics, such as in South Korea and America; and a Christian song-and-dance troupe who shout during alley performances, "It's the power of the Holy Spirit! Nothing can stop it!"

"Jesus in China" also pointed out the country's Bureau of Religious Affairs, and lawyers who specialize in religious freedom issues. Interestingly, many Chinese credit the 1989 Tiananmen Square incident as the catalyst that turned tens of thousands of disillusioned young people all across China towards Christianity. What a remarkable fulfillment of Romans 8:28 that reminds us God can bring about good for His Kingdom from any situation!

Several months ago, I heard about a church congregation in China that numbered around two hundred when my family lived there and worked with them pre-1950. Today the congregation numbers more than 1000 and praises God for a new church building. It's just like the Apostle Paul said, "Christians plant and water, but God gives the increase" (I Corinthians 3:6).

Today, Chinese no longer taunt Westerners in public by calling them "foreign devils." And in spite of decades of atheistic Communism, God's increase in China has happened in amazing ways. So how can I not give thanks to God and share some of my family's and friends' part in the growth of God's Kingdom in China!

This Great Wall photo on the front and back covers was taken pre-1950 by Millie's father, Fred Nelson. He was a lifelong missionary in China and Taiwan, and a Marine Corps captain interpreter for intelligence in China during WWII. Fred is the inspiration for the character Alfred Newquist in the published *Hungry River* and *Dragon Wall* historical novels, and the yet-to-be published novel, *Jade Cross*.

Dragon Wall:
A Great Wall Novel

Prolog

Abbie's Journal
September 11, 2002

. . . *OH GOD, OH DEAR GOD – how well I remember Mom moaning that prayer over and over when her anguish in war-ravaged China was too great to bear. On today's unforgettable anniversary, I too moan the terrors of war. At the same time, I'm so proud of America, so grateful for the heroism of Americans here and overseas. This evening, some news clips from Hussein's Iraq were shown on CNN, declaring Americans live in fear since 9-11 last year, and our leaders too. Those poor, deluded people – they just have no concept of our vast freedoms and power and fearlessness, nor of our lack of ambition to conquer for the sake of conquering. . .*

. . . *on my desk, I have a daily reminder from my China boxes of the dreadful cost of conquest. It's a piece of the ancient Great Wall – one of Grampa Nils's precious mementos, passed on to Dad and now to me. Whenever I hold it in my hand, I ponder its history. Not long ago, I read online many Chinese can't understand the fascination of foreigners for the Great Wall. Sure, they're glad for the tourism money it brings. But to them the Wall is a symbol of unimaginable oppression and conquest. Let it crumble and fall away – they say – it's a reminder of millions and millions of tragic deaths.*

Living my childhood in the shadow of the Wall, I often heard its dreadful stories. Like my young Chinese playmates, I thought of it as a huge dragon, a twin to our family's dragon Yangtze River – as both could be fearsome and mysterious, and not to be slighted for fear of what might happen. . .

. . . several months ago, I read a touching Wall story by Jim Clayton in his book, Who Is Going to Heaven. *His story goes something like this:*

Centuries ago, one of China's emperors spent his entire reign expanding the Great Wall to keep barbarians out and his subjects in. Millions of men and lads were conscripted and sent north to the Wall as laborers. Few ever returned home, and the wailing of wives and mothers could be heard throughout the provinces. Wall laborers daily witnessed horrible deaths, then were forced to pound the bodies into the Wall along with stones and clay. No one had friends for long, as few survived the torturous conditions.

One day a man noticed the friend who slaved beside him was shivering and staggering. Ai yah – he mourned – I am so sorry. He took off his tattered outer garment and put it on his friend. And he worked harder so the guards wouldn't notice his friend was scarcely working.

That evening, his friend was too weak to stand in line for the small portion of rice gruel and tea allotted to each, so the man brought his own portion to his friend, and went hungry and thirsty. Though exhausted, the man stayed awake during the night to comfort his dying friend. In the darkness before dawn, he struggled to bury his friend's body in secret and thus appease their pagan gods. But alas, he was discovered and brutally killed by the guards.

Meanwhile, on the other side of the world, an Irish Christian monk who spent his days in a monastery fervently *praying for the heathen and carefully copying the Holy Scriptures to save them for future generations, wrote these words of Christ – I was thirsty and you gave me water to drink. I was hungry and you fed me. I was cold and you gave me your garment. You did all these for me. Now welcome home, my deeply loved and worthy friend. You will share in my Kingdom forever and ever.*

. . . wow, what a story – as the Chinese say, one to ponder for ten thousand fragrant years. It's no wonder the Great Wall, like the Great River, is one of China's dragons. . .

PART ONE

1933 to 1938

The Great Wall's starting point, Zhendong Gate, in Hopeh Province. The gate is also called Shanhai Pass (way through). The characters read: "First Pass Under Heaven."

Chapter 1

Abbie's Journal
Oct 10, 2002
. . . today is the Double Tenth – a holiday like a Nationalist Chinese Fourth of July. And I understand better than many what it stands for. My family lived through those decades of bloody revolutions, riots and wars. Lately I've been thinking I should do something meaningful with what's in my family's China boxes. Maybe even write a book. Scary thought, to be sure! But why just stash away my journals and other writings along with those of my parents and grandparents? If I don't do something with our China stories, who will? And in time, some descendant or stranger will throw away our boxes of aging papers – like I almost did before my amazing trip back to China two years ago. . .

Shanghai, China, 1933
Year of Rooster

Every few minutes, the young female mourner paused from her loud wailing. She wiped her sweaty face with a grimy cloth, and peeked curiously at the people crowded along the street watching the funeral procession.

This was Li-ming's first experience as a paid mourner in Shanghai, and she was hot and sticky in the stiff white mourning robe and hood covering her patched, dirty clothes. But she barely noticed her discomfort as she gazed at the amazing city where she had arrived just yesterday by ox cart.

Weeks ago, she and her cousin had disguised themselves as boys and run away from their ancestral home in the remote village of Twentieth Tower Gate of China's Great Wall. Soon to be married to aged widowers, they had both agreed in secret they would rather die escaping than live forever miserable. And so one moonless night, they fled from the serpentine shadow of the Great Dragon Wall. Their cash dowries stolen from their families were securely hidden in their undergarments.

After weeks of perilous travel, the two had arrived at Shanghai's West Gate. They were dust-covered and hungry, their dowries nearly gone. There the plump manager of the Shanghai Sang-fu Mourning Company, with a leering smile, offered them food, work and housing.

Li-ming had looked briefly at her cousin before nodding a silent acceptance for both of them. She desperately hoped their work as paid mourners would soon erase their impoverished past and, in time, enable them to repay their dowries to restore honor to their families. Following the manager, Li-Ming had rejoiced with her cousin at this seeming good fortune bestowed to them by fate.

As they hurried past a small streetside shrine on their way to the Mourning Company, she had said, "Stop, Cousin! We should do a quick thank you *bai bai* worship to the god here."

"But is this the deity of our village?" her cousin had questioned.

"I don't think it matters," Li-Ming had replied. "If we want our good fortune to continue, we should *bai bai*. This may be our only opportunity today."

Using one of their last small coins to purchase an incense stick from a beggar monk seated beside the shrine, Li-Ming did not notice the aging wooden idol looked at the two of them with stony silence. She and her cousin were used to that. Nor did they know the idol failed to warn them that paid wailing by day would soon be accompanied by far worse duties at night, and that now their chances of survival were few. With hope for the future, they had knelt before the blackened idol and touched their heads to the ground.

*   *   *

As the newest mourners, Li-ming and her cousin walked last in the long funeral procession. They followed dozens of other paid mourners, a sign of the deceased's family's wealth and status. Ahead of the mourners, Li-ming could see the musicians, whose flutes and strings sounded a dismal dirge, with occasional pauses for piercing clangs from cymbals.

In front of the instrument players, the family idols were paraded on the shoulders of coolies. These fierce-faced statues, clothed in soot-darkened silk brocades, rode haughtily on black and gold sedan platforms. The pungent smoke from rows of incense burning before each idol wafted backwards. Shaven-headed priests and monks in their best yellow and red robes escorted the idols, along with idols rented from the city's largest temple.

Following the idols were numerous ox-drawn carts loaded with extravagant food offerings. Li-ming had heard other mourners comment that Fan Merchant was making sure the funeral of his number-one wife made up for his well-known neglect during her life. He obviously had no intention of being avenged by her unhappy ghost.

I would not mind being neglected, Li-ming thought, *if my husband had money. Besides, if I did not like him, I would want him to have others and not bother me.*

In front of the idols, the ornately painted, black lacquered coffin swung heavily from a stout wooden pole, balanced on the shoulders of coolies. Six in front, six behind, the men wore identical white mourning robes and headbands. From time to time, the coolies paused from the weight of the load, wiped their faces with new sweat towels, then chanted together as they resumed their swaying march.

Accompanying the coffin were coolie-pulled carts carrying fancy paper houses, paper servants, and other paper effects to be burned at the deceased woman's tomb for her use in the after-life. These were lavish works of art, and onlookers gasped at the splendor soon to be Mistress Fan's. When Li-ming viewed these earlier, she had whispered to her cousin that maybe they could become second wives or concubines of rich men. Her cousin had glumly replied they were not pretty enough. And besides, they had ugly, large peasant feet.

"With pretty clothes and styled hair, we could be pretty. And I have heard large feet are becoming fashionable," Li-ming had whispered back, self-consciously smoothing her black braids, unkempt still from lack of washing and combing during their flight.

When she heard the mourners near her whisper that the young man leading the procession was the departed woman's only surviving child and unmarried, Li-ming stared openly at him. Dressed in obviously costly clothes under his mourning robe, he carried his mother's elaborately framed portrait with dignity as he strode down the street. He cried out and struck his chest in grief at appropriate intervals. His father followed, seated in one of the family's gleaming black and chrome private rickshaws, pulled by a uniformed servant.

Behind Fan Merchant and the idols came dozens of other family members, relatives and friends. The strong, younger ones walked. Older men, women with bound feet, and middle-aged women with half-bound feet rode in sedan chairs carried by servants or in hired rickshaws.

*   *   *

Unknown to Li-Ming and her cousin, they were observed by two young women staring at the procession from the doorway of a cloth shop on Nan Ching Dong Lu Street.

"*Wah!*" the first young woman said to her companion. "See those last two? They are the newest mourners, are they not? They look like ignorant country girls, same as we once were. We must tell Lin Teacher about them as soon as we get back to the shop. Maybe she will find a way to rescue them in time like she did us."

A few minutes later, the two young women were startled to see someone else of interest in the crowded street. A large, elderly foreigner with eyes closed sped past them in a rickshaw that nearly bumped into them.

"*Hai,* careless coolie! Watch where you are

going!" the second young woman shouted.

The foreigner jerked his shoulders, but didn't open his eyes to look at them. If he had, he would have seen the startled look on their faces.

"*Wah!* Do you think he is the husband of the benefactor of Lin Teacher?" the first one asked.

"Yes, yes, he looks like the man. He looks like the foreign man in Lin Teacher's photographs, the one who lives in her home village far up the Great Long River. I wonder if she knows he is here in Shanghai?"

With news of such importance to tell their teacher, the two cut short their outing. They hurried back to the studio shop where they were apprentices to an esteemed scroll artist. They discussed hiring a rickshaw, but decided instead to save their precious coins, and walked quickly to their teacher's residence where they lived in her apprentices' dormitory.

*   *   *

Abbie's Journal
Oct 24, 2002

. . . an article I read in the newspaper yesterday sticks with me – about a retired teacher who volunteers in public schools. He said good memories help children have good lives. So he wants to give children good memories, partly by telling them stories from his life. That impressed me – and strengthens my resolve to share my family's China stories. We've had more than our share of tragedies and hard times. But God's grace was always with us, helping us survive and overcome! And our lives in China were often adventurous and wonderful – so unlike the missionary story of Barbara Kingsolver's Poisonwood Bible *– which made me so angry when I read it and its rave reviews! Yes! I want to tell my family's story to bring balance to her appalling one. . .*

Chapter 2

Abbie's Journal
Oct 26, 2002
. . . crazy I know, but I still think of the Yangtze as my family's river, even though poor Mom hated it. I guess I feel this way because we have had such a long association with it – so many fascinating experiences and stories. Like the river people, we often called it the "dragon river." We didn't superstitiously fear it like they did, but we often were afraid of its violent ways. And it's still a dragon river – just this week Chinese news estimated that multiple thousands have died from recent floods and mud slides. Makes me wonder if today's river dwellers, after decades of atheistic Communism, still try to appease the river gods. I didn't see any evidence of worship rites along the river during our recent trip. But next trip, I'll pay closer attention, and ask. . .

Shanghai, China, 1933
Same Year of Rooster

The lean, muscular coolie firmly held the long pole handles of his rickshaw as he ran towards the Bund. His passenger leaned back against the cushioned seat, eyes closed. A lifetime spent in China, and still Nils preferred not to see the dangerous congestion the daring coolies darted through. Rickshaw rides often made him dizzy and anxious.

Today Nils was also weary. He had slept only in

brief spurts for several nights, pondering how to tell Alfred and Meggie his decision.

What a way to welcome my son back to China, he thought, *and Meggie his dear wife. But at least Alfred isn't alone this time. Oh please, Almighty God, grant them the assurance of your grace. Ja, just as you did for my Lizzie and me time after time. And thank you, thank you for your ever-present and ever-great faithfulness.*

Just thinking about Lizzie caused Nils to feel the now familiar pangs of sorrow and loneliness.

Ja, how I miss her. I'm too old and too alone to serve here in China any longer. Is that your release, Almighty God, for what I think I should do? If it's not your will, grant me a clear sign. And please, please help Alfred and Meggie understand.

Even with his eyes shut, Nils could sense the rickshaw was nearing the river front. The chants and shouts of cargo coolies became distinguishable. Sharp odors from the river overtook those from the open street-side gutters. As always, he swallowed repeatedly, fighting nausea.

For forty years, he had recoiled at the stench of the Bund waters. He had not become accustomed to it – no matter how hard he tried, no matter how fervently he prayed. So, long ago he had accepted this ugly part of life with stoicism – with the stoicism of a Chinese gentleman.

And no wonder I respond like my friends here, Nils thought. He paid the coolie and handed him a Gospel tract. Ja, *decades of living here have made me feel more Chinese than American or even Swedish. When they call me white Chinese, they're nearly correct.*

He walked towards the dock assigned to Alfred

and Meggie's ship, looking with revulsion and sadness at the filthy waters swirling against the Bund. How he wished his efforts to clean up the river had been heeded by someone in the government. It was such a dreadful source of disease.

Perhaps Alfred will be more successful, he thought. *Perhaps I should encourage him to do what I've refused to do, give some red envelopes, and think of them as gifts not bribes.*

Seeing the ship was still far off, Nils strolled farther down the Bund, his teak cane steadying his stride. Remembering, he prayed for those in the funeral procession that had interrupted his rickshaw ride earlier. From appearances, the deceased was not a believer in True God. But who could know for sure? The woman whose photograph he had glimpsed may have been a secret Christian, and maybe some of the family mourners were too. They had plenty of money for Western opportunities – that was obvious.

Thinking about the procession caused Nils to reflect as he often did how funerals without the hope of eternity with God always had an aura of darkness and desperation. Well, that's why he had lived most of his life in China, wasn't it, to bring God's light and hope? But had he done enough? Had he made enough of a difference?

He considered these disturbing questions briefly, then allowed memories of previous occasions on the Bund to engage his thoughts. As a young seaman from Sweden, this was where he had renewed his promise to God, forever changing the direction of his life. Left here by his merchant ship because of an accident, he had met Lizzie, a young Salvation Army captain. They fell in love while she nursed him back to health. Long voyages for their family to and from Sweden and America had begun and ended here, with many tearful goodbyes, as well as happy welcomes – like today's.

Nils stopped to rest in front of a large building with stone columns and a tile roof. Smaller, similar buildings showed above its walled courtyard behind it. When he closed his eyes, he could imagine the old sign in front with the words, "Gospel Hall," instead of the present sign, "Chen's Import and Export Company."

He thought how surprised passersby would have been to know that he, the tall elderly Westerner pausing there, owned the place. And that today he was glad he and Lizzie had leased it years earlier instead of selling it. Now the property was extremely valuable and worth far more than all its troubles over the decades.

Several week ago when Nils had received a letter from Iowa with an unexpected message from Oliver, he knew the time had come to sell his Bund place. For Oliver needed his help – kind Oliver who had helped them in so many ways for so many years. At last Nils could do something in return for Lizzie's special friend since childhood, the man his children loved and called "Uncle" Oliver, and whose name Lizzie had given their third son.

* * *

Alfred and Meggie leaned against the ship's railing. They watched the buildings of Shanghai's Bund loom larger and larger. Suddenly, Meggie began to sob. Alfred looked at her in surprise. He was so intent on coming into harbor, he had almost forgotten her there beside him.

"Why ever are you crying, Sweetheart?" he asked softly, not wanting the other passengers around them to notice.

"Oh, Alfred, everything is so strange and so awful. Just look! Can't you see what I mean?" She gulped. "Can't you smell it? I'm almost afraid to breathe and look." She lowered her head onto her arms resting on the railing and kept sobbing.

"Hush, Meggie! Others are looking at us. What will they think?"

"I don't care. I shouldn't have come. I shouldn't have married you. All I ever wanted was to be a nurse and wife and mother. But back at home, in America. You know I never wanted to come here. I don't want to live in this strange place. I just want to go home."

Alfred put his arms around Meggie to soothe her. Then he guided her down the stairs to the cabin they shared with three other couples. He hoped the others were all on deck.

Thankfully, their shared cabin was empty. He gave her a wet cloth for her face, then sat close beside her as she lay on her bottom bunk.

"Meggie Sweetheart, I think you just feel this way because you're pregnant and you've been so seasick. I think you'll soon be fine, and you'll be happy here. You know, I've heard both Mama and Papa tell about feeling the same way you do when they first came to China."

She gulped several times before stammering, "Really, Alfred, did they really?"

"Yes, especially Papa. Sometime soon ask him to tell you the story of his arrival. Even though it was years ago, things haven't changed much. And he still dislikes coming to the Bund. I'm sure even today, even to meet us. He calls it a cesspool. I guess because I grew up here, I don't notice it as much. To me it's just the Bund and this is how it is. I know Almighty Lord God will help you bear it, just like He did Mama and Papa."

Alfred hugged his wife, caressing her tenderly. He didn't tell her he had been so afraid this might happen. How he had prayed she would feel love for China like he did. Nor did he express his deep pain to be coming home knowing his mother would not be at the dock to meet them.

In his heart, he prayed yet again with desperation. *Almighty Lord God, grant Meggie a heart for China. Help her to be as brave as Mama. And help me to be as strong as Papa.*

After a while, Meggie stood up, a tiny, stiff smile on her face. "I feel a little better. Thank you for understanding, Alfred. No wonder I love you so much."

She leaned over and kissed the top of his thick, wavy hair. He stood up too. And then it hit him. Meggie smelled like flowers, a familiar delicate fragrance. He was too shocked to say anything. Later he would tell her about his mother's sign of grace from God. Could it be God had sent the sign of that special grace to Meggie as well, and as a comfort to him?

Thank you, Almighty Lord God, he said over and over in his heart as they climbed the stairs and resumed their place on deck.

Meggie shaded her eyes from the sun with her hands and solemnly watched the ship dock. When Alfred spotted his father Nils and waved and shouted excitedly, she too waved and called out greetings with a brave smile.

Though her face kept smiling during their first weeks in China, Alfred sensed her heart was weeping. He felt keenly her private struggles with homesickness and an intense dislike of their new surroundings.

But a month after their arrival, everything changed when he placed their tiny, newborn son into Meggie's arms. Alfred watched the tears of relief and happiness flow down her face and onto Donny's tiny head. As he hovered over them, Alfred smelled again the gentle fragrance of flowers.

Lord God Almighty, he breathed prayerfully, *thank you, thank you, for making your wonderful grace known to Meggie – and to me.*

The next evening as they lay on their bed with Donny snug between them, Meggie whispered, "Alfred, something wonderful happened to me yesterday. I can't explain it, but I'm not homesick anymore. Oh yes, I still wish so much Dad and Mama and the others could see darling Donny. But it's just a wish, not a longing filling me with terrible pain."

"I'm so glad, Sweetheart," Alfred said. He wanted to ask her about the fragrance, and tell her about his mother's experience. But the words didn't come, not this time. Maybe another time.

* * *

Nils stayed long enough in Shanghai with Alfred and Meggie to embrace his first China-born grandchild, and to escort the young Newquists to visit longtime family friends, including Lin Hui-ching, the painter of scrolls.

They enjoyed a delicious feast in Hui-ching's gracious apartment above her studio shop – a celebration to welcome Alfred and Meggie, and a farewell for Nils. Highly regarded for her exquisite scrolls and calligraphy, with these dear friends from her youth, Hui-ching was not a Shanghai art master. With them, she was a humble daughter and sister.

She laughed with delight and clapped her hands to see Alfred again, and to meet Meggie and darling baby Donny. She mourned and shed tears with them as they remembered Lizzie with loving stories. And Hui-ching told Meggie how the Niehs, especially Lizzie, had opened the difficult doors for her to education and art.

Late in the evening, Hui-ching brought in her apprentices to meet these foreign friends who were like family. She introduced them, saying, "Because of you, my Nieh benefactors, I now open doors to a good life for these young females. I do this to honor you, and to bring honor to the memory of my mother and sister. Some would say to appease their spirits."

As the apprentices were leaving, Hui-ching called to the last two to stay for a minute longer.

"These are my newest apprentices," she said with a kind smile and touch. "They come from a Great Wall tower village far away. Thanks to you, I can give them the opportunity to be artists instead of mourners by day and red-district girls by night."

After the young apprentices left, bowing and backing away, Nils said to Meggie, "Later I'll tell you more about the wonderful work Hui-ching is doing. She is saving these girls from unspeakable lives – and deaths."

As Hui-ching and Nils said farewell to each other, to his surprise she said, "I've always wanted to see America. Now you will be there, so perhaps I will visit. I would like to see your family's country. And maybe there, I will be brave enough to become a public follower of True God. I know you have prayed for me to have courage for this for many years."

"That would be so wonderful," Nils said, his tired face showing his delight, as he clasped his hands together and bowed. "Every day I pray you will allow True God to direct your eternal destiny before it is too late. Please do not disappoint my children and me. And remember, I will always treasure the beautiful scroll of the Yangtze River gorge you gave my wife. Thank you, thank you for honoring my family with your achievements."

*   *   *

Once Nils was satisfied he had fulfilled his parental and property obligations, he prepared to sail away from the Bund for the last time. He was heading for Iowa to live with Oliver on his farm near Des Moines, with gratitude in his heart that Alfred and Meggie eagerly supported his decision to help Oliver save his farm.

Yes indeed, Nils reflected, as he tucked in the mosquito net around the bed for his final night in China. God had guided their family's endeavors in this land. The Bund property had sold in two days for even more than anticipated. With a portion of the proceeds,

Nils could now pay off Oliver's indebtedness from the Depression years.

In addition, he could live the last part of his life on Oliver's farm as a helper, not a burden. They would be company for each other in old age. They had so much to remember together. And Nils had always wanted to do some farming, or better yet, tend a small orchard. Most of all, he wanted to live without the never-ending sorrow of death and destruction caused by wars and floods and famines.

He was also leaving enough money with Alfred and Meggie to support years of mission work. Gratitude swelled inside him that he would still be a part of God's Kingdom in China, both through his children and through his stewardship.

But before he settled in Iowa, Nils was looking forward to a visit to his roots in Sweden. How good to see his relatives and friends there one more time. After Sweden, he planned to tour the Holy Land – a pilgrimage he and Lizzie had long promised themselves. He had failed to find the Stone Ten Keepers for her, but he would visit the Holy Land in her memory. And maybe, just maybe, Alfred would one day find the mysterious Stone Ten Keepers that had eluded Lizzie and him for so long.

As he said farewell to China, Nils's greatest sadness was leaving behind three family graves in the Sian Christian Cemetery. There, not long ago, he had buried his beloved Lizzie beside their Hilda and Oscar, both children murdered in the dreadful 1911 Sian riot. How he would miss the comfort of praying at their graves and touching their names on the stones.

"Won't you also miss Fengshan and the river?" Alfred had said the evening before he left while they talked together with missionary friends in the cool courtyard of the mission station hostel.

"Ja, I suppose," Nils said slowly. "But only because they were home for so long. Son, I am so tired, tired to death of calamities and wars. Now the Japanese are threatening all of China, and Chiang and Mao are making the Chinese fight against each other. I can no longer bear the suffering. But you are young and hopeful like I once was. I thank Almighty God for giving me peace that it's time to pass my mantle to you – and from Lizzie to you, dear Meggie."

He laid his hands on them both and turned his face up towards heaven. He wanted to pray aloud, but his emotions were too strong. So he reached to God from his heart. For several minutes, a holy hush filled the courtyard. Even the children and servants around them stood motionless.

*   *   *

The next day, Nils stood on the deck of his departing ship, his arms lifted upwards. As he looked down on those biding him farewell, the span of murky water between the Bund and the ocean liner gradually grew greater and greater. The silhouettes of Alfred and Meggie and the others on the wharf faded fainter and fainter – but not the power God in his heart, nor in theirs, he fervently prayed, his lips silently moving.

*   *   *

Abbie's Journal
Nov 7, 2002
. . . late last night, I finished reading Keys of the Kingdom

by Cronin for the first time. I wonder why I haven't read it before – I've known about it for years. It's a wonderful novel, and so true to life. I'm amazed how similar the China experiences of Father Francis were to those of my parents' experiences. I admire how he and my parents were alike in their kind manner, and how they were not pushy in their Christian witness. Plus they were so determined and sacrificial in their lives as they endeavored to improve the lives of the Chinese in whose midst they lived. Catholic or Protestant – in eternity it's not going to matter, as long as our hearts are right before God through the mystery of Christ. And it's great when people live that way on earth – like my parents and Father Francis, like we all should. . .

Chapter 3

Abbie's Journal
Nov 10, 2002
. . . *I was reading in Donny's baby book today and remembering about Mom telling me years ago how her love for China was a miracle. At the time, I was moaning about a terrible time in my own life. So she told me about a terrible time in hers, and about trusting God more than she ever thought possible. It started right after she gave birth to Donny. She said she hadn't spoken of the experience before, only Dad knew a bit about it, but even he didn't know all of it. As Mom shared with me, a delicate fragrance wafted around her, and a wonderful feeling of the almightiness of God filled me. Wow – I still get the most peaceful feeling just remembering. Ever since then, I've trusted God more fully, and applied Romans 8:28 more completely to my life. . .*

Sian, China, 1934
Year of Canine

"We should arrive very soon now," Alfred said to Meggie.

They stared intently through the train window. Outside, the rain streamed down the glass, distorting their view of the passing scenery. Alfred's movements revealed his excitement. Meggie hoped the woman he lovingly called Mother Ruth had received his telegram and would be at the station to meet them.

"She's like a second mother to me," he reminded

Meggie. "All those times she was with my family when we suffered. I don't know what we would have done without her. We would have been like lost puppies."

Meggie nodded from habit and smiled. She had heard the stories before.

Alfred continued, "I remember the time we went back to Sweden with her after Hilda and Oscar were martyred. Every day on the ship, she consoled us and found interesting things for us to do. And helped our feelings towards the Chinese, too. I'm so thankful she was here to help and comfort Papa when Mama died. I'm sure she'll want to take us to the cemetery one of the first things."

Alfred spoke so calmly, but his comments like this always made Meggie nervous. She wondered what had it felt like being there when his brother and sister were gruesomely killed by rioting Chinese, and barely escaping himself. Alfred rarely spoke about it.

And how did it feel to be going to his mother's grave for the first time, and to remember being so far away when she died he couldn't even go to her funeral? Whenever Alfred talked about his mother, Meggie could tell he had adored her. Meggie didn't like to have to think about death, especially now she was here in China, so far from home and her family. But it was an inescapable part of her life with Alfred.

To cheer herself, she looked down at little Donny sound asleep in his basket between them. The train had soothed him like a giant rocking cradle, and he had slept most of the trip. As she checked to make sure he was okay, Meggie wished she was the one stretched out in a warm bed sound asleep. She wondered if she would ever feel rested again. Being married and having a baby was more tiring than she had ever dreamed.

The train began to slow. Even in the rain, groups of people stood along the tracks, their strange-looking rain hats and coats dripping water. In a few minutes, the train hissed to a stop in the station. The wooden platform was crowded with hundreds of people, but at least they were dry under the high tile roof.

"I see her! I see Mother Ruth! Look over there!" Alfred pointed to the left side of the platform. "She's waving her scarf. See her?"

His father's exuberant voice awakened and startled little Donny. But Meggie let him cry for a few moments while she tried to get her first glimpse of the woman she seemed to already know without having met.

"I see her too!" she said with sudden excitement, her voice matching Alfred's.

She quickly bent down and picked up Donny. "Look, Donny," she said, pointing. "There's your Gramma Ruth! See darling? See?"

Alfred looked at her with surprise. "Why, Sweetheart, what a good idea for Donny to call her Gramma Ruth. She'll be delighted. And how she'll love him. Having no children of her own must be one of her sadnesses."

Meggie's eyes filled in sympathy for the special woman she was about to meet. Humming and smiling, Alfred didn't notice as he stroked their son's soft cheeks and hair.

*   *   *

"I can hardly believe you're really here," Mother Ruth said to Meggie and Alfred the next morning at breakfast. "Especially you, Meggie. I could probably write a book with all Alfred has told me about you, his girl with the Irish name, not a Swedish name like most of us. How he missed you and longed for you those years you were apart."

"I was missing him, too, terribly!" Meggie said. "And I also have a hard time believing I'm finally here in Sian. Of course, Alfred belongs here. See how bright and happy he looks? My mind wants to belong too, but my heart still gets so homesick. I don't know when my folks will get to see our son."

She blinked rapidly, and looked down at little Donny squirming contentedly on her lap. Mother Ruth's and Alfred's eyes followed hers and looked at him too. Donny responded with laughter and baby chatter and waving arms.

"I guess he feels like he belongs," Meggie said and lifted her face to Mother Ruth. "It must help to be born in China."

"Maybe," Mother Ruth said. "But I must confess to you, my dear. After all these years, I still have days when I ask God why I'm here."

Alfred jerked his head and looked at her. Then he said, "Does God answer you?"

"Always!" she said, her eyes shining with faith. "But not always right away. I'm sure your own mother would have said so too. Thinking about her, shall we visit the cemetery today, maybe after lunch while Donny is napping? My housegirl can take care of him if he awakens before we return."

Meggie looked at Alfred. They hadn't left Donny with a Chinese servant yet. But she knew the time was coming and her pulse quickened.

"Not yet, please," she signaled with her eyes.

"Yes, of course we want to go today," Alfred said to Mother Ruth. "But let's go this morning. I want to take Donny. Don't you think so too, Sweetheart?" He laid his hand on Meggie's arm to reassure her.

"How do we get there?" Meggie said, relieved about Donny.

Alfred looked at Mother Ruth with raised eyebrows.

"We'll go by rickshaw," she said." The coolies won't mind waiting for us at the cemetery gate. They know we pay extra if they wait. If it's all right with you, I'll send word to other missionaries to join us. Then we can have a special little memorial service. That will be good for you, for all of us."

Suddenly, Mother Ruth was overcome with weeping. She covered her face with her hands and her napkin. Alfred and Meggie wept too.

When she had composed herself, she said, "*Oh min min*, I miss dear, dear Lizzie so much. And now your father is gone too, and I'm missing him. But I'm comforted because I know one day we will be together again – in Glory – and there God will take away all of our sorrows forever."

"Amen," Alfred said.

"You sounded just like Nils," Mother Ruth said sadly. "Well, let's get busy and we'll feel better. We should try to leave in an hour. And when we get back, Alfred, remind me to get the trunk your father left here for you. I expect he told you in Shanghai. He wasn't sure when you'd be able to get to Fengshan. He especially wants you to look at your mother's notebook about that ancient monument and the Stone Ten Keepers."

"He may have mentioned the trunk," Alfred said. "But I don't remember him saying anything. Do you, Meggie?"

She shook her head, then said, "Who are the Stone Ten Keepers? Are they dangerous?"

Alfred shrugged his shoulders. "We don't know who they are for sure. But for years, Mama was keen to find out about them because of their old friend Wu Headman. She had some interesting guesses about them. They seem to be connected in some way with the ancient Nestorian tablet. Maybe because it has a small cross engraved on the top."

Mother Ruth nodded. "I'll take you to see the monument, Meggie, whenever you like. We've all seen it here in the museum. We don't have time now since we're going to the cemetery, but later I'll tell you how we found the monument. Years ago it was Lizzie who insisted we look for it. What an adventure! We went all over the countryside in donkey carts, and it was right here in the city all the time."

She rang the bell for the housegirl to clear the table, and hurried to the back courtyard where the houseboy was working. She sent him with a message to the houses of several other missionaries. It was a message she had told them to expect.

*   *   *

The rickshaw ride to the cemetery was Meggie's

second chance to take a look at Sian. And yesterday scarcely counted. For when they rode to Mother Ruth's from the train station, she had not focused on the city and its people because Donny was fussing. Today he sat happily on her lap and looked around with her. The people they passed stopped whatever they were doing to stare at them. When they saw Donny, they laughed and gestured, saying things Meggie didn't understand. But she smiled and nodded, especially to the women with babies tied on their backs.

They make me feel like I live the life of a princess, she thought.

But the feeling changed when dozens of ragged, sore-infested beggar children began running after them, reaching out with filthy hands to touch Donny and to beg for money. Meggie recoiled, protecting Donny with her arms. In halting Mandarin she told the rickshaw coolie to run faster. At that, he turned his head towards the children and shouted something at them.

Immediately, the children stopped their chasing. Meggie wondered what the coolie had said. Probably not something very Christian, she worried and felt guilty, but also safer. The rest of the way, she rubbed Donny's soft hair with her chin and bemoaned the plight of all those poor, poor children.

*   *   *

Pulling her nightgown over her head and down her body, Mother Ruth sighed and sighed again. She crossed the room and tucked in the white mosquito net carefully all around her bed except for her crawl-in spot. She turned out the oil lamp on the dresser and quickly got into bed, hoping no mosquitoes or other night bugs had come in with her. She lay still listening. No, she didn't hear any bugs whining or moving.

Thank you, dear God, she prayed. She was extra tired tonight, and thankful not to have to swat in the darkness at bugs caught inside her net.

They're both so sweet, Meggie and Donny. Thank you, dear God. And thank you for a day without the sounds of war, for the special time this morning in the cemetery. I'm so glad Alfred and Meggie are finally a family. Oh dear God, please protect sweet, sweet little Donny. I love him already. Thank you for this loving couple you've blessed me with. They're like my own children.

She dozed a bit, then murmured, *In Jesus' name, Amen.*

Wearily, Mother Ruth turned onto her side. Maybe tonight God would let her dream about Bertil. When she dreamed of him, which was rare anymore, for days afterwards she was uplifted by happy memories from their married years. Seeing Alfred and Meggie together reminded her of her long ago loss – and of Nils's more recent one. Thinking of poor Nils also reminded her she'd forgotten to give Alfred the trunk of Lizzie's things.

Tomorrow morning, right after breakfast, she thought. *I'll get it for him right after breakfast.*

*   *   *

Abbie's Journal
Nov 22, 2002
. . . I'm so excited! Dan and I are going to Ireland next August. He's earned one of his company's luxury trips. It's a country I've long wanted to visit – partly because of Mom's stories about her father's stories. I vaguely remember visiting

Grampa McIvers *when we lived in the States. It was WWII and Dad was still in China as a Marine interpreter. But I didn't get to know Grampa M well. By then, he was too old to voluntarily tell me his Irish stories or play his spoons for me, and I was too young to know to ask him. There's a McIvers castle not too far from Dublin. Maybe we'll get to see it. Interesting, Dad traveled to Sweden to check out his family's roots, but Mom never went to Ireland. I wonder if she wanted to. Probably not, since her Irish roots go back several generations more than Dad's Swedish ones. . .*

Chapter 4

Abbie's Journal
Dec 3, 2002
. . . Uncle KP and Aunt Lou visited last weekend. They're just back from their first trip to Ireland, and had fascinating photos to show us – wow, perfect timing, since we're going too in a few months. I can sure tell Mom and KP had the same father. They both have his famous storytelling skills. KP told us some great stories from Ireland, and about the McIvers still living in the legendary family castle. Sounds like the current heirs are afraid we American descendants might want a share of the castle. They made sure KP knew our ancestor was disowned in the 1700s. We don't know many of the details of the disowning, but supposedly a son back then fell in love with a girl from the wrong church. KP couldn't remember if the son was Catholic and his lover Protestant or the other way around. Whichever, their families disowned them, they eloped and came to America, and he ended up fighting in the Revolutionary War. I wonder if Dan and I will get to see the castle when we go. . .

Fengshan, China, 1935
Year of Boar

"Warfare," Alfred muttered, staring at the devastation along the banks of the river. The line of trackers chanted in unison as they heaved on the rope pulling his family's aging Good News Boat upriver.

"All China has known is bloodshed and more

bloodshed, plunder and more plunder! And now when Japan is more cruelly aggressive than ever, the poor struggling Republic keeps breaking into civil war."

"Fu-de, my good friend, are you speaking to me?" the young boatman said loudly from his position at the junk's large wooden tiller. "Or are you praying to True God for our protection?"

Alfred moved closer to stern of the boat and the boatman, restlessly running his hand through his wavy brown hair.

"No, Young Chu," he said in fluent Mandarin, "I was not talking to you or True God. But I should be praying. I am so distressed to see the destruction of the town we are passing. Who do you think is responsible this time? The Japanese army?" He paused. "Maybe Mao's soldiers? Or possibly Chiang's? But I hope not his."

"Maybe none of those," the adopted son of old Chu Boatman said. "I think river bandits or maybe a band of rebel soldiers. Perhaps this river town did not give what was asked in food or money. See that banner hanging on the tree by the smashed gate? I cannot read the characters from here, but I have seen other bandit warnings looking like it."

Alfred lifted his binoculars to his eyes and looked at the banner, then up at the hills behind the river town.

After a few minutes he said, "Are we in danger from attack too, do you think?"

"No, Fu-de. Have you forgotten the gunboats not far ahead of us and not far behind? You have seen how your country's boats patrol the river with fearsomeness these days. I am not afraid when we are flying your American flag for protection."

"That's exactly what I was saying to the wind earlier," Alfred replied. "War, war, and fear of war. Your great country is being destroyed by too much fighting."

Young Chu nodded. "Of course, you are right. It is because so many men's hearts are evil with greed, both foreigners and also my own countrymen. Not enough men follow the ways of True God. You must preach more, like your father used to."

Alfred smiled and nodded. "And you too, Young Chu. You must tell about True God whenever you can. Your people will listen more earnestly to you than to me and other foreigners."

Neither man spoke for a while, then Young Chu said, "Since the light from the sun will soon be gone, shall we not stop at the next town for the night? The trackers are hungry and tired from pulling all day. I know you hoped to get to Fengshan before dark, but you have seen how the swift currents from the rains have slowed us. But I think we can still arrive by the noon rice tomorrow."

*   *   *

Long after the exhausted trackers and boatmen had fallen asleep on the dock where the boat was tied, Alfred kept watch from the roof of the main cabin.

Just like Papa used to do, he thought, thankful God had called him to follow in his father's footsteps.

On this night, he even had one of his father's old guns hidden in his sleeping bag beside him. He wondered if Meggie felt as strongly against guns as his mother had. If so, she hadn't said anything when they found two of Nils's guns in the trunk left for them with Mother Ruth. He had meant to ask, and then had forgotten as they continued looking through the trunk, their interest taken by his mother's notebook about the Nestorian monument and the secretive Stone Ten Keepers who were mysteriously linked to it.

"Of course, I want to help you find them," Meggie had said to Alfred after they read some of Lizzie's notes. "Your mother's words make me curious too. I'm astonished by the mystical and spiritual effect the stone tablet had on the man she calls Wu Headman. It's amazing how God works, isn't it?"

Alfred sighed several times. He was missing Meggie and little Donny on this trip. Uneasy, he stood up and looked for signs of movement along the river and in the sleeping river town. Even though the night was moonless, he could see everything was as it should be. Relieved, he stretched several times and sat back down in his folding chair. Judging by the stars, Young Chu would soon be taking his place so he could crawl into his sleeping bag for a few hours.

His thoughts drifted again to the Stone Ten Keepers. He was eager to search for them, and remembered the times as a child and a young man when he had helped his mother in her search. He was glad Meggie seemed interested. The mission council had recently granted them permission to search during evangelistic convoys. But first, he was taking several months to check on the mission work in Fengshan and the surrounding stations.

For years, Alfred had looked forward to living in

Fengshan with Meggie in his parents' Great House, the one place he considered home. But it turned out Meggie was too afraid to travel on the river. Twice she had boarded the Good News Boat with him and Donny, along with all their luggage and supplies. And both times she had become frantic not long after they started out, causing him to tell the boatmen to return to shore. He had hoped her fear was just because she was pregnant again.

So he had delayed going to Fengshan, and taken her and little Donny on the train back to Sian and Mother Ruth. Several days later, he had returned to Cheungking and set out for Fengshan alone with his boatmen and the hired trackers who would pull them upriver.

Now after a month on the river, he was nearly back home. Soon he would be feasting and laughing and singing with dear Fengshan friends he hadn't seen for three years. Of course, they would be so disappointed Meggie and Donny weren't with him. But they would understand. There were river people who, like Meggie, were afraid to travel on the river even though they lived beside it. But no doubt they would be surprised a foreigner was afraid, especially one who was Alfred's wife and a believer.

* * *

"You see, I was right," Young Chu said to Alfred. "We are here in time for the noon rice." He smiled broadly as he pulled hard on the tiller to direct the boat to Fengshan's ancient stone wharf. The trackers were bent nearly to the ground with the strain of pulling the boat around the gorge's last sharp curve.

"Yes, yes, you have excellent knowledge of the river," Alfred said. "Your father, old Chu Boatman, taught you well. He taught me well too, like an uncle. It is sad for me to think he died two years ago and will not be here to meet us today."

"I miss him too, my foreign brother. But how can we be sad for my father who is now in heaven? Ah, look, look! The people of Fengshan are rushing out to meet you. Although my father will not be among them, my mother will be. She is a happy old woman – especially today, because you are like a son to her and she has been hoping to see you before she dies."

"Why have you not told me she is unwell?"

"She seems well, that is why. But she is old, you know that. And she talks often of death and joining your mother and my father in heaven."

As Alfred and Young Chu watched, hundreds of villagers gathered on the ancient stone wharf. Some quickly descended the stone steps to the dock. Suddenly, the Temple gong sounded three times, and then three times again.

"*Ai ya!*" Young Chu said. "That is not a welcome for you. It is the warning signal that dreaded soldier conscriptors have been sighted. I must hurry and hide with the other young males and females in our secret tunnel or risk being kidnapped. *Ai ya!* Pray for us, Nieh Friend. Right now, pray aloud so all can hear."

Alfred climbed quickly to the roof of the main cabin. At the same time, Young Chu called to an older man on the steps who traded places with him at the tiller as soon as the boat touched the dock.

"What about the hired trackers and polers,"

Alfred called urgently to Young Chu who was running up the steps.

"Tell them to hide if they can. You know they cannot come with me and the others to our town's hidden refuge."

"Go with the protection of True God!" Alfred called back.

As the boat was tied into place and dozens of young people were disappearing, Alfred raised his arms and head towards heaven in prayer. In flawless Mandarin, he cried out to True God to protect Fengshan and especially the town's youth at this dangerous moment. He prayed also for the hired trackers and polers under his care, and for wisdom for them all. Hundreds of voices fervently joined his "Amen."

Then he stepped down from the cabin and onto the dock. The townspeople who remained clustered joyfully around him. For long minutes, they carried on as if nothing else was happening. But as soon as they heard the anticipated racket of horse hoofs on cobblestones, they quieted and looked towards the street beyond the wharf.

There four men jerked four war horses to a clattering stop. The leader shouted, "Your headman, where is he? I demand to speak with him."

An elderly man stepped forward from the crowd. "Yes? What have you to say to me?"

"You should know," the leader of the conscriptors shouted back. "You should know I am here to give your young men the opportunity to serve our country."

The leader looked around. "Where are your young men? Call them forth."

The headman said, "They are gone."

"Gone where?"

"With young men, who knows for sure?"

"*Hai!* Do not mock me," the leader rebuked. "It is my duty to get twenty strong soldiers from your town, either by choice or by force. If not young males, then young females. If I do not get them, I will order twenty of you beheaded. If I get them, you will be rewarded with protection."

The leader waved his gun over his head, and the men with him shouted threateningly. Their horses snorted and stamped.

To the surprise of the conscriptors, the townspeople facing them showed little fear. Instead they turned around and looked at Alfred.

"Ah, so a foreign devil has just arrived," the leader said, eyeing Alfred. "Now I know why you are gathered here on the wharf. We thought perhaps you had been warned of our coming."

No one moved or said anything, except for Alfred who walked closer to the mounted men, his hands behind his back.

When he stopped in front of them, he said, "I may look foreign to you, but I am not to these people. I grew up in this town. My family named Nieh is well-known in this area."

"Ah, you speak our language with ease," the leader said.

"Yes, and I know you have no legal right to kill any of these people. The headman has told you the young men are gone, so go on your way. Although I was born here, America is my country. So this town has the protection of America. Do you not see the flag on my boat?"

"Where are those who would protect you and these people?" the leader taunted. "They cannot catch us regardless of what we do."

Alfred quickly brought his hands in front of him, and pointed his father's gun at the leader. "I too can kill," he cried out, startling the men and their horses. "But I hope not to because I am a man of peace, not war. But if you do not leave at once, I will shoot my gun into the air. Do you know who will respond? The nearby gunboats of my country. What do you think the soldiers on them will do to you? Do you think they will give you the chance to leave unharmed as I am?"

*   *   *

All that afternoon and evening, Alfred celebrated with the townspeople their escape from the conscriptors. The storytellers among them told their favorite stories of past times of protection and escape, stories in which Alfred's father Nils and mother Lizzie were often the heroes. Even those in hiding took turns coming to the celebration feast in the headman's courtyard. But they were careful, for who knew how long it would be until they could live freely and openly again with conscriptors roaming the nearby countryside?

The celebrations noises were heard by boatmen passing on their junks through the rushing, turbulent waters of the Fengshan gorge. Later, a watchman on the wharf told Alfred and the headman that he overheard one boatman call to another, "Hear those festival sounds? I have heard those who live here are followers of a foreign god's religion. But they seem happy and prosperous, even though the rest of us are not during these fearsome times of war. On our return trip, let us think of a reason to dock here and question them, shall we not?"

Alfred nodded and smiled, and the headman said, "The Spirit of True God is working in their hearts." Bring those boatmen to me when they stop here.

*   *   *

Abbie's Journal
Dec 15, 2002
. . . a book I ordered from Amazon just arrived, Dragons on Guard: An Imaginative Interpretation of Old China. *It's my Christmas gift to myself. Dan likes to tease that I keep Amazon in business – ha! This book has some of the old legends I heard from my childhood Chinese friends – fun memories, for sure. One of my favorites is in the book, and I*

read it first – the one about why the eastern tip of the Great Wall has been called a dragon's head since the time in ancient days when that part of the Wall gobbled up big-nosed barbarian foreigners as if it were a real dragon. The barbarians were frightening people who looked like my family, my friends used to say, and I laughed with them at their joke. When I got older, I realized they probably weren't joking. The Chinese sometimes laugh at things that aren't funny. . .

Chapter 5

Abbie's Journal
June 1, 2003

. . . *Phil and I don't know when Dad became an informer for the American military, but based on hints in his journals, it was probably several years before the Marine Corps requested him to serve as an interpreter in China during WWII. He was so fluent in both his spoken and written Mandarin, he was often called a white Chinese. It appears he continued informing for a number of years even after we fled the Mainland and settled in Taiwan. In hindsight, I can see he must have traveled on some extremely dangerous, secret missions in China for the American military while the U.S. was still backing Chiang Kai-shek.*

. . . *now that I've read his journals, I wish I could ask him or Mom some questions – like who was the lady on a stretcher he helped rescue from the Japanese and secretly transported down the Yangtze on our Good News Boat? Was she really Amelia, the Amelia Earhart, as I remember hearing him and Mom whisper? To my great surprise, when I toured AE's home in Atchison last week and told the elderly docent about my recollection, she said what I heard as a child probably did happen. She believed the China theory, and said there was a telegram to prove it. She was convinced AE for some reason lived incognito after returning to the States. The docent was sure she had personally shown an aging AE around the home. She said only AE could have known to ask some of the questions that lady had asked. . .*

Sian, China, 1936
Year of Rat

Meggie carried little Kilby in one arm. With her other, she guided Donny as he hopped along beside her. The earth they crossed in the courtyard was packed down hard and smooth, except where bushes, flowers and trees grew. Meggie was still getting used to the Chinese not liking any grass in their gardens.

Afternoons were her favorite time of the day. Her morning hours of tedious language study were over, and the boys were just up from their naps, happy and playful. When the three of them reached the center of the garden, she sat down on a carved stone bench by the fish pool, settling Kilby on her lap.

"Come here, Donny, and let Mommy fix your arm guard," she called.

Donny came obediently, laughing and talking about the funny fish playing in the water. He looked at her with his large brown eyes. She tugged the cardboard guard back into place over his left elbow and gave him a quick hug.

Then he threw the bits of bread from his pocket to the goldfish already swimming round and round in anticipation. Baby dragons, she had heard Chinese call them, and wondered why. Maybe tonight she would remember to ask Alfred.

Whenever Donny played outside the house and sometimes even inside, Meggie made sure his little elbows were inserted into cardboard cuffs so he couldn't put anything germy into his mouth. Another missionary mother had suggested the cuffs to her. With her medical background, the idea seemed sensible, though Alfred and Mother Ruth were dubious. But so far, the cuffs seemed to be working. Donny hadn't had any of the terrible dysentery so many young children died from, both Chinese and Western.

She rubbed her chin gently back and forth on the top of little Kilby's soft head. He was eight months old already, and soon she would be putting guards on his chubby elbows too. At moments like this, how she longed for her family so far away to be able see and hold her lovable darlings. But that wouldn't happen for years yet, since missionary service terms were for ten years or more.

After a while, little Kilby became restless and wanted down. So Meggie called out in her halting Mandarin to the houseboy who was taking down the dry laundry, "Tang Brother, please bring me my baby's buggy."

"No, Mommy, not him. I want to get it for you and Kibbie," Donny said, running to her.

"Why of course. You're such a big boy now and my good helper. You can get it."

Donny started towards the back porch, then turned around and called back in clear Mandarin to the houseboy, "I am getting the buggy for my little brother. You do not have to help me. I am big now."

The houseboy laughed and clapped his hands as he nodded to Donny.

Meggie sighed. The Mandarin language was so difficult for her. At three, Donny already sounded Chinese, just like his father. She was so proud of him. At the same time, she wished she could learn Mandarin as easily as he had.

She watched Donny struggling to push the bamboo buggy with its wooden wheels towards her. It was a little taller than he was, and he had to peer between the slats to see the path.

Alfred should be here to take his picture, Meggie thought, walking slowly to Donny with Kilby waving his arms and leaning towards the buggy.

"Hey little one, you're sure getting big," Meggie said to him.

"But I'm still more big, amn't I?" Donny said.

"You'll always be his big brother, and he'll always be your little brother," Meggie said, giving Donny a quick hug.

She sat Kilby down in the buggy. Immediately, he grabbed the bamboo rails and pulled himself up to a standing position, jabbering to Donny. Meggie smoothed her dress and put her hands on the handle beside Donny's.

"Let's walk over to Tang Brother and talk to him while he folds the clothes," she said.

"Yes, Mommy. He can help us practice our Chinese. I like him. He's fun."

Meggie smiled. She must remember to tell Alfred and Mother Ruth at dinner tonight what Donny had said. She knew they would chuckle too.

* * *

That evening at dinner, Alfred seemed preoccupied. He smiled occasionally, but mostly he was quiet, unlike his usual talkative self. Meggie wondered if he had heard more dreadful war news, but she didn't want to ask during the meal because of

Donny and Kilby. Then as they lingered over tea while the housegirl was clearing the table, he made a startling statement.

"I think I've discovered where we can find some Stone Keepers," he said, his eyes bright as he looked back and forth between Meggie and Mother Ruth.

"No! Have you really? I'm flabbergasted!" Mother Ruth said. "Why, for the longest time you've not even looked or asked about them. I can't recall you mentioning anything since your return from Fengshan last year. And I've tried hard not to pester you."

"Oh, but I've been looking and asking," he said, grinning a bit smugly. "I just haven't reported anything. With all the war hostilities throughout the area, I've had to be very careful. I've been protecting the one who's been giving me information."

"Such good news, Sweetheart!" Meggie smiled, her brown eyes intent on him. "I'm excited for you and for all of us, and for your mother too. I wish she could be here to see the look on your face this moment. I just hope what you've discovered isn't going to involve something so dangerous and secret the boys and I can't join you, like most of your trips."

"It's a different kind of secret trip this time. It may be a long one. But it'll be a land trip, not a river one. We'll travel by donkey cart and sedan carriers. Maybe even our bicycles. I think you can all come along, because it will also be a preaching, medical trip. And we'll distribute New Testaments, too."

"Sounds complicated," Meggie said, "and seems like you've already done plenty of planning – without us." She frowned for a few seconds, but soon her eager look was back.

"But where is it you're going?" Mother Ruth said. "Can I come too, or do you think I'm too old to travel to wherever it is you're going?"

"No, you're not too old. I think you can make this trip, but I can't tell you where we're going. This way, no one can force either of you tell. And everyone involved will be safer. Also, the Stone Ten Keepers, whoever they are, won't be warned about us coming. I guess you'll both just have to trust me, and God."

Alfred moved from his place at the end of the table to Donny's empty chair beside Meggie. He said, "Sweetheart, I haven't done much planning at all yet. I've just barely started thinking about some possibilities. In fact, I'm like both of you. After so many years of being mystified, I find it difficult to believe we may be close to finding out something. I've been longing to find out the truth for Mama and Papa's sake, and for myself too. I'm afraid if we don't check out this lead right away, we may never get to if the fighting gets worse."

Mother Ruth said eagerly, "If we can find out the truth before I retire next year, then I'll for sure visit Nils in Iowa on my way home to Sweden and tell him everything. So I do want to go along, even though it may be hard on my old bones. Besides, you'll need me to help care for little Kilby and Donny, and to keep the coolies behaving."

She laughed joyfully. Reaching over the table, she took one of each of their hands in hers and lovingly squeezed them.

"Let's go to your office, Alfred, and work on

travel lists right now, shall we? As soon as Donny and Kilby are asleep, you can join us, Meggie dear."

"I will if I don't fall asleep with the boys," Meggie said. "And if I don't join you tonight, there's always tomorrow."

She excused herself from the table and walked over to Donny and Kilby who were playing in their toy corner. "It's time to pick up now, darlings, and hug Daddy and Gramma Ruth goodnight," she said.

Later, reading a bedtime story to her sleepy sons, Meggie pondered if she and the boys really should go along on this strange trip with Alfred. Traveling in China these days could be so hazardous, especially with young children. There were germs everywhere, and who knew where the next deadly bombing or conflict might burst forth. Plus there were always bandits lurking along travel routes. She tried to suppress a feeling of foreboding.

Oh God, oh dear God, guide us, please especially guide me, she prayed silently. Aloud she prayed with her young sons:

> Now I lay me down to sleep.
> I pray the Lord my soul to keep.
> If I should die before I wake,
> I pray Thee Lord my soul to take.
> Amen

*   *   *

Abbie's Journal
July 18, 2003
. . . Lisa See's memoir about her Chinese-American family is terrific! I'm rereading On Gold Mountain *for some book*

reviews I'm doing on her first novel that's just out, Dragon Bones, *set along the Yangtze. She sums up so well Japan's final aggressive moves on China with these words: "On July 7, 1937, Japan suddenly mobilized its impressive war machine, attacking and seizing nearly all coastal cities and industrial areas, effectively closing off China from the sea. These events persuaded Mao Tse-tung and Chiang Kai-shek to put aside their own bitter disagreements temporarily and fight together against their common foe." Those war years were so horrendous for my own family, but they were also years of amazing blessings. . .*

Chapter 6

Abbie's Journal
Aug 6, 2003
. . . *I have heaps of little travel notebooks Dad kept – of his trips up and down the Yangtze, along the Great Wall, and to many other places. And I do mean* little *notebooks. They were small enough to fit in the pockets of his shirt. Some he bought, but many he made himself. Each cover is labeled with his name Alfred Newquist in English and Chinese. His writing is always tiny and neat, sometimes in a shorthand that left out vowels and unnecessary consonants. Dad's little notebooks contained expenses and other lists, sermon outlines, Bible verses he was memorizing, recipes, information interesting to him, daily travel distances and happenings, and so forth. When I read them, I can hear his voice again, see his alert, happy face, and feel his tremendous enthusiasm and energy. . .*

Along the Great Wall
Northern Shensi, China, 1937
Year of Ox

For two weeks, the convoy of mule-drawn carts and sedan chairs had made its way over the rough roads and trails bordering a section of the Great Wall, and even atop the wall a few times. Six armed guards took turns riding two horses, and occasionally shooting their guns into the air to scare off bandits and renegade soldiers.

The small convoy was headed towards a

destination known only to Alfred.

Each afternoon about four o'clock, he stopped the convoy for the night, and sometimes for several nights depending on the location. They camped when there was no inn or temple available to house the missionaries and their children, the guards, servants, and a dozen or so mule cart and sedan chair coolies.

Whenever a crowd of Chinese gathered to watch them, they held a Gospel service. If the crowd responded with sincere interest, they stayed in that location several days and nights to hold more services, and to have medical clinics. Alfred, with his dental training, was the one who extracted rotted teeth and treated mouth abscesses. He stitched up severe cuts and set broken bones with the help of Mother Ruth and Meggie, who also dispensed medicine and advice to the women and children. Elmer Anderson, a new single missionary assigned to work with Alfred and Meggie for a year, helped hold the patients being treated, as they had no painkillers, nor did the Chinese expect painkillers. Elmer also handed out tracts and practiced his Mandarin to the great amusement of the gathered Chinese.

Before they traveled on, Alfred gave a New Testament to someone who could read Chinese characters, or who said they knew someone who could read. The honored individual would be encouraged to read aloud to the community at least once a week and preferably on Sunday. Alfred was always touched to see the New Testament carefully wrapped and respectfully carried away.

So far, Alfred thought, as he strode beside the

cart carrying Meggie and the boys, the trip had been gratifying. Pleasant surprises and miracles kept them all buoyed by a constant sense of God's presence and guidance. God was using them to touch people physically and spiritually. Nothing really terrible had happened.

But the next day, things suddenly changed. Very early, as the sky above them was turning from black to gray, several coolies came to him with the bad news that three of the mules had disappeared during the night. They did have two extra mules for rotation and emergencies. Even so, losing three mules would leave one cart without a mule.

"Thank you for telling me right away," Alfred said to the worried coolies. "I will pray about this, and then we will trust True God to help us solve this problem. It is dangerous for us not to have enough mules. But those who took them may be even more dangerous."

"Yes, yes, we hoped you would not be angry with us, but instead pray to your god, the one you call True God," one of the coolies said.

Alfred prayed while the coolies listened. Then he told Mother Ruth, who was also up early, what had happened. To her, he dared expressed his frustration God had allowed this to happen.

"God will take care of it," she said. "Of course, it's inconvenient and the coolies might have to pull the cart until we can buy some new mules. But you know, Alfred, God might return our mules to us in time to pull the carts, and at the same time touch someone with his love."

Alfred smiled at her and nodded. "You're right, of course. I should accept what God allows with more trust. I'm thankful for your strong faith, Mother Ruth. I hope my faith will one day be as strong."

"Well, you know what the Bible says about that," she said. "Trials develop our faith. I have had far too many in my life, and I still wonder the "why" of some of them. You're in a trial right now. But this trial is also a chance for the coolies to experience God at work with something affecting them. We must pray especially for them, that their darkened hearts will turn to the light of God."

By breakfast, everyone knew about the missing mules. Soon Donny was repeating in his cute Mandarin what he was hearing, "Our mules are gone. What shall we do? Our mules are gone. What shall we do?" Then he added, "I know. Daddy, you go find them. Go now."

Alfred stopped eating his cooked millet cereal and looked intently at his young son. Then he said to Meggie, "Out of the mouth of babes – actually, I hadn't thought of looking for the mules. But if I do, where should I look?" He smiled at Donny and went back to eating.

Meggie stood up with little Kilby in her arms and shrugged. Alfred could see worry on her face. She walked over to their mule cart. It looked like a small covered wagon, and she had fixed up the inside as a cozy traveling spot for her and the boys. She put Kilby inside so he could toddle around in cleanliness and safety.

She came back to their table, a clever folding table of light-weight bamboo that Alfred had shown a local carpenter how to make. She helped Donny finish his breakfast, then walked with him back to their cart so he could play with Kilby while she talked with Alfred and Mother Ruth.

"I'm afraid bandits are following us, aren't you?" she said. "Who else would dare steal our mules?"

"What I don't understand," Alfred said, "is why all the coolies agree they heard nothing. How could they not have? There must have been some kind of unusual noise. Something's not right."

"They're not telling the truth," Mother Ruth said. "They were either threatened or bribed."

"How about the guards?" Meggie said. "Which ones were supposed to be on duty last night? I was feeling pretty safe before, but now I don't. I want to go home, Alfred. We have to think of the boys."

"We'll reach our destination in another day or two," Alfred said. "So I sure don't want to turn back now. Besides, I don't sense fear of bandits in the coolies. Something else is going on. I think I'll do what our wise little Donny said. I'll search for the mules."

"Who will you take with you?" Mother Ruth asked.

"One of the guards and I can ride the horses. That will be the safest and fastest. Whoever took the mules can't be too far away. If we don't find anything, we'll return in a few hours and decide what to do next. If we find the mules, I'll shoot my gun twice, and then twice again. If I shoot only once, Mother Ruth, that will be your signal to send Elmer and some others to help."

Mother Ruth nodded, then said to Meggie and

Elmer, "Let's have a morning service while Alfred's away. We all need to strengthen our faith, and pray for him. And this time, I insist you play the accordion, Meggie."

"I haven't played one before, remember?"

"But you can easily learn because you play the piano so well. It seems to me today is a good time for you to start. No one out here except Elmer and me will know the difference. And you have such a lovely, strong singing voice for leading singing, just like dear Lizzie. Next year, I want to leave my accordion with you since we don't know what happened to Lizzie's."

Mother Ruth helped Meggie put the accordion on and fasten the back strap. She showed her which buttons to push for the main chords, and then went to the cart where the Donny and Kilby were. When Meggie started playing, she told the boys to look at what Mommy was doing. Soon everyone was singing along with Meggie, or at least trying to, the words of her favorite hymn:

> Blessed assurance, Jesus is mine.
> Oh, what a foretaste of Glory divine.
> Heir of salvation, purchased of God,
> Born of his Spirit, washed in his blood.
> This is my story, this is my song,
> Praising my Savior all the day long.

While they sang, Alfred and one of the guards rode off on the two horses. Nobody paid much attention to them because it was a daily sight. What Meggie was doing was far more interesting, partly because she didn't take part in services as often as Mother Ruth. His wife's lovely voice followed Alfred, and he felt a surge of encouragement lift his spirit. "Amen!" he said loudly in Mandarin. "Praise God!"

The guard following him echoed his words, but only to be polite and with far less fervor.

After they gone down one hill and up another, the guard pulled his horse up beside Alfred and said, "I think I see caves over there behind those trees. If I stole mules, maybe I would hide with them there until the owners traveled on."

"What if bandits have the mules, or even renegade soldiers?" Alfred said.

"No, I see no sign of bandits or soldiers. The way we are traveling now is seldom used since the new road was made alongside the railroad tracks. These days, there is nothing on this side of the mountain to be plundered. But perhaps these caves were once used as hideouts."

"Then let us go and look," Alfred said. He headed his horse in the direction of the caves and readied his gun.

*   *   *

Mother Ruth was telling a second Bible story message, the story about the Good Samaritan, when she stopped abruptly. "I just heard two gun shots," she said to Meggie. "There, two more. Thank God! That means they have found the mules."

She smiled at the Chinese clustered around her and continued the story. When she had finished and answered everyone's questions, Meggie played the accordion again and led the group in singing a song they all knew well because they sang it every service:

Lai shin Ye-su.
Lai shin Ye-su.
Come believe Jesus.
Come believe Jesus.
Right now, come, believe Jesus.

Later, when she was putting the accordion in its case, she said to Mother Ruth, "You're right. It isn't hard to play. And playing and singing have helped me stop worrying. There's something so holy and uplifting about Gospel music, isn't there?"

Mother Ruth nodded, looking at her with puzzlement for a few moments before she said, "Do you smell flowers? I don't see any, but I smell a fragrance."

Meggie nodded and looked away. A few seconds later, she picked up the accordion case and handed it to Mother Ruth.

"Thank you for encouraging me to be the one to play this time. And listen, I don't hear anything from the boys. They must be napping. Stories always put them to sleep," she said, smiling. "I think I'll stretch out with them until Alfred and the guard return. I wonder where they found the mules, don't you?"

"We'll soon know. I'm going to give the cook instructions for the midday meal now. Then we can get on our way sooner."

When Alfred and the guard arrived back at the campsite, to everyone's surprise they each had a young lad riding behind him. They also had the three mules in tow. Meggie, Mother Ruth, Elmer and others from their group came quickly to where the men were dismounting.

"I cannot believe it! Are these the thieves?" Mother Ruth said in Mandarin.

The two lads lowered their heads in fear and shame. They were skinny and dirty, wearing tattered clothes and worn straw sandals.

Alfred put a hand on each lad's shoulder. "They are sorry for stealing our mules," he said. They have agreed to work for us to pay for their wrong doing. You will hear the whole story. But first, I want them to wash up and get dressed in some better clothes. When we eat, I tell you what I know."

Usually the midday meal was a noisy one.

The coolies and guards liked to argue loudly while they ate. Alfred and the other missionaries always had plenty to discuss too. They sat at their folding table. On the other side of the camp cooking stoves, the Chinese squatted on the ground in small groups to eat. Most of the time, they all ate the same simple meal of rice or noodles with stir-fried vegetables, peanuts and tofu, and occasionally tasty pieces of chicken or pork.

Only little Donny and Kilby had meals especially prepared by Meggie, supplemented with goat's milk, boiled and then cooled, or when that was unavailable, powdered milk mixed with cooled boiled water. For an occasional treat, the missionaries enjoyed cups of instant coffee mixed with milk and sugar instead of the Chinese tea everyone drank.

Except for the smacking of lips and the clicking

of chopsticks, the meal after the mules and their thieves were found was unusually quiet. Everyone wanted to hear Alfred tell the story of the two strange lads in their midst, and how he and the guard had found the mules.

"The guard with me was the one who saw the caves," Alfred started. "Even though we both carried guns, I was hesitant for just the two of us to look there. What if we were ambushed by a band of rebels or bandits? But our guard here was braver than I. He said he saw no signs of anyone."

The other guards and coolies admired Alfred's admission. They cheered for their friend, and those near him playfully punched him on the shoulders.

"I wanted to shoot our guns into the air to instill fear if someone was around, "Alfred continued. "But of course, we could not do so because we did not want to send wrong signals to you back here."

Everyone laughed.

"The first two caves we looked in were not deep. We could see they had been lived in, but not recently. The third cave we looked in was deep. We could not see any mules or anyone else, but we could smell mules and hear muffled sounds from far back in the darkness. Guard called out fiercely for the thieves to come forward with our mules or suffer consequences. Imagine our surprise when these two lads came forward. They would not speak to us. So we brought them along and told them we would feed and clothe them if they worked hard to pay for their wrongdoing. I think they will talk now. They look better, and I am sure they feel better since they have eaten and learned we are kind Christians. They know now we will not beat them nor cut off their hands for stealing."

"Come," Alfred said to the two lads. "Come and stand by me. The time has come for you to answer our questions. And I expect you to tell the truth."

The two came and stood beside him, their heads bent and their hands nervously grasping their unfamiliar clothes.

"How old are you?" Alfred said.

The two looked up at all the eyes staring at them and then at each other.

The larger one answered, "We do not know. Maybe he is twelve and I am fourteen."

Alfred asked next, "Are you brothers?"

Again the larger one answered, "We think we are brothers because we have always been together. We do not remember our parents or any other relatives. As long as we can remember, we have lived by begging or stealing. Some older people in the town over there," he gestured in the direction Alfred's convoy was traveling, "told us our parents died during the last famine. But how can we know?"

"Is the town Twentieth Tower Gate?" Alfred said, his face and body tensing with eagerness.

"Yes! You have heard of it?" the younger one asked, surprised.

"We are going there," Alfred said to the lads, and then again to everyone gathered around listening intently. "Yes, that is where we are going. I can hardly believe these two are from there. How amazing! How wonderful!"

"But we still don't know why they stole our mules," Meggie said to Alfred. "Ask them."

"Yes, of course, I almost forgot in my excitement," he said, then asked them Meggie's question.

"We often stay in these caves," the older one answered. "Not many people travel this way now. But when they do, they often camp here like you have. It is easy to steal from them at night. Just like it was easy to steal your mules. Whatever we steal, we sell in the village after the travelers have passed through. You are the first to catch us. Because of bandits, other people are afraid to search the caves for what they have lost."

Mother Ruth checked the sky and then said to Alfred, "Are we going to stay here another night, or shall we travel on? We need to decide because the day is passing. And I suggest we should travel on."

"Yes, good thinking. Let us pack up to travel on," Alfred said to everyone.

"Can we reach your village before the sun is gone?" he said to the lads.

"Yes, yes," they both said. "But we are wondering why you foreigners have traveled so far to come to our village. It is a nothing place."

"I have heard some Stone Ten Keepers may live there," Alfred said, running his hands through his wavy hair. "Do you know about them?"

The two lads gasped and covered their mouths with their hands. They shook their heads and were silent. When Alfred questioned them again, the older one said, "We have nothing to say. We can say nothing. You must ask the headman these questions, not us worthless beggars."

*   *   *

Sian

Several weeks later, the convoy reached the mission station in Sian. The return trip had been much the same as the outgoing one, except they no longer had a sense of excitement. To their great disappointment, beyond what the beggar boys had said, they had not found out anything about the Stone Ten Keepers. Their search had ended just like Lizzie's during the years she occasionally searched for them.

When they had reached the town of Twelfth Tower Gate with the two beggar boys, no one, not even the magistrate, would discuss the Stone Ten Keepers with them, not even when offered payment. The only responses to their questions were blank looks and shrugs.

Outside of that, the magistrate had treated them as honored guests, with feasts and Gospel meeting privileges. They had stayed a week before heading back to Sian, taking the beggar boys along to enroll at one of their mission schools for orphans. During the farewell evening with the town, the magistrate had gratefully and with many bows received a New Testament.

The first day back on the road, Alfred asked the others if they had noticed the strange look in the magistrate's eyes when he was presented with the New Testament. The others had not, but agreed that what Alfred had noticed seemed significant.

"I want to go back in a year or two," Alfred said. "Maybe next time, they will trust us more, and someone will tell us something about the Stone Ten Keepers."

"Whatever mission I'm stationed at when you go back there," Elmer said, "please include me in your convoy. Even if you never find the Stone Ten Keepers, just think of all the Chinese people who hear the Gospel during trips like this."

For several days after their return to Sian, the trip and the Stone Ten Keepers dominated their mealtime conversations.

During one of those conversations, Mother Ruth said, "If I've left China by the time you go, be sure to write me. I've become as curious about them as dear Lizzie was. I'm sure glad I could go with you on this trip, especially since you'll be moving soon to serve in Kien-yang. My, how I'm going to miss all of you! But what great experiences we've shared together, praise the Lord!"

* * *

Abbie's Journal
Aug 22, 2003
. . . after BT died, I didn't write much for months. BT was my closest writing companion, always at my feet as I wrote – and grieving for her stilled my creativity, even my journal writing. At times I wondered if I would write anything again besides letters and emails. If losing a beloved Chow affected me so deeply, I can only imagine what losing sons did to my parents. They left a record of their grief in their letters and journals – a record I couldn't bear to read for decades, and can scarcely read even now, 70 years later. But when I do read letters like the one Mom wrote when Kilby died, I'm in awe at God's grace evident in their lives – and how God used their suffering to bring many, many Chinese to belief and hope. Wow, what a heritage! I'm so thankful for their faith and courage, and grateful they passed some on to me. . .

The Nestorian Monument from the eighth century proclaims Christianity. This photo was taken outside Sian in the early 1900s. Research reveals that the Jewish and Christian faiths have been present in China for more than 3000 years.

Chapter 7

A letter home from Meggie
Kien-yang, near Sian, China, 1938
Year of Tiger

July 28, 1938
My own dearest Mother and Dad and Mother Ruth
(carbon copy),
You, of course, have already received Alfred's
telegram of our sad sad news, but I want to write you
more of the details of what God has permitted to come
into our life – and has been indeed the hardest thing God
has ever asked me to bear.
Just last Friday during the week when we were
here alone on the mission station with both our servants
gone, we were so happy. I mentioned to Alfred that was
one thing we missionary women missed, keeping our own
little homes. So I was enjoying it so, more real bodily
exercise, and I had fixed Chinese character lists here
and there to study while I was washing dishes, making
fires, etc. I also mentioned to him I hadn't taken the
time I should just to enjoy my babies, but did the
necessary things, then left them to play. So I had taken
little Kilby into the parlor and just sat and rocked him,
with his little face to mine and he and I enjoyed it so. I
called out to Alfred, "He certainly is a healthy little
rascal, isn't he?" Alfred answered that Kilby was surely
healthy, but he wouldn't stay a rascal.

That very night at midnight, Kilby awakened and cried so hard. I found he had had a very loose stool and it was irritating his little bottom. I knew he was cutting teeth, so gave him Chloroidine right away, and after changing him, walked the floor with his little face on mine and he was soon fast asleep.

But Saturday, more loose stools. So I gave him castor oil right off and then more Chloroidine, and fixed him in his little bed part time and part time out in his buggy. From the very first, he just slept and slept and seemed very weak. I remarked what a good patient he was, letting him sleep, going about my work, but running to him at the least cry and sitting by him. We thought his sleeping was good, for it would reserve his energy. But we believe now it was because of his extreme toxic condition.

Saturday I cleaned the whole house and washed clothes.

Sunday to my surprise about twenty children came for Sunday School. None have been coming all during the hot, busy farm season. I hurriedly got the benches, and thinking Kilby was sleeping so well, taught the lesson which for Sunday in our leaflets was about the woman who brought her little girl to Jesus and He healed her. I told the children God could heal, and hoped He would heal my little one also – for God knows how many times I took him on the wings of prayer to my Savior.

Sunday we had guests as we had planned, and they were much surprised to discover I could make Chinese food. We had a good time and felt it good to let people know we could carry on without servants. Several saw the baby. In the evening, I didn't go to the service, but carried little Kilby in my arms about the courtyard. He was so listless and weak, and I said I hoped he didn't leave us for heaven. Someone said I mustn't talk like that. He was just weak from teething, loose stools, and the heat.

Each night we kept a lamp low, and I on our side of the bed just next to him was up four and five times. But always after being nursed and cleaned, he fell immediately off into such a deep, deep sleep.

Monday he seemed so much better, and several times he had formed stools. That was what puzzled us so. We remembered Donny's stools when he was sick with dysentery, and Kilby's stools were never half as bad – not once a tinge of blood, and only a bit of flim the first two days. By Monday night I was getting weary, but I slept well and little Kilby exceedingly well. He only awakened once. He was covered each time I looked at him, and in such a deep, peaceful sleep.

His not being decidedly better on Tuesday made us search again the doctor books, and we decided it was some fever. But such a sudden onset and no constipation could not ring clear to typhus or typhoid fever. We thought perhaps it was a relapsing fever, and would just take days of careful nursing. We considered going to the hospital in Sian (and how I wished we had been there like we were when Donny was so sick), but two days journey there in the extreme heat and with all the war turmoil made that seem unwise. So we dismissed it.

Tuesday morning I was studying with my language teacher by Kilby's bed when he became restless and it soon took on the picture of pain, so I said of course I could not read anymore and took little Kilby in my arms. During the remainder of the day, he had about ten spasms of real pain and would cry out. I feared convulsions, but thank God he spared our darling of that and us of that sight.

Alfred was at the jail service when Kilby's pain started, but I gave him paregoric as we had once before and he grew quieter as I walked him in my arms. When Alfred got home, there were signs of more seriousness. And many times in the next few hours with Kilby in my arms, his daddy and brother knelt by us, encircling us in their arms. Through our tears we asked to be willing for God's will, but in our humanness, if possible to spare the little life we loved so much. I wish now instead of being glad for the stoppage of the stools, I had realized it was not right and had given him an enema. But how could we know, when that was one of the signs we had hoped for. Early in the morning we had seen two or three little red spots on one of his wrists, but no others on his body anywhere. We never had to force fluids as with Donny. I hadn't been giving him powdered milk, for I remembered with Donny it seemed to upset his stomach and come through in big curds. That was why I was still nursing little Kilby this summer, even though he was teething and would sometimes bite so hard.

About noon we decided to call for a Chinese doctor someone told us about who is here caring for wounded soldiers. He came within an hour, with an assistant and two nurses. They had every sign of knowing just what they were about. The doctor looked in his throat, and did a careful exam with the stethoscope all over Kilby's lungs and stomach.

The doctor laughed a hearty kind laugh. He said we were good parents and just a bit too frightened. It was just a little summer stomach epidemic and good nursing was all that was needed. His temperature was then 102, so the doctor sent back some Salol. We were so happy, we brought our fried chicken dinner in by little Kilby's bed and ate, for we had not wanted food before.

But very soon Kilby seemed to get cold. Putting warm water bottles around him, we became truly alarmed and gave him the second hypo of heart stimulant. We tried to give him some herbal soup one of the church deacons brought. But just then he vomited with a spouting brown fluid. I tried to nurse him, but he didn't seem himself and would not suck and bit me fearfully.

We were in despair, but asked God to help us be strong. We sent for the doctor again. He came immediately and said to give another heart stimulant which we did. We turned little Kilby on his side, propped him with pillows and sat very close with our arms all about him. But soon his eyes seemed set and his breathing a bit harder. Before we could do anything, so quietly and peacefully his little chin dropped and it was all over.

My Bible lady, the evangelist's wife, and other dear Christian Chinese lady friends wanted to bathe and fix him for us. But I told them I had done it many times and was not afraid. Together we fixed him all up – put his little woolies on him, a pair of bright little Chinese stockings, a diaper, then his little blue silk Chinese gown and the darling Chinese cap that you, Mother Ruth, gave him just before you left China. We carried his limp little body out and placed him on the padded board we use for ironing on top of two benches out in what we call our ting fang, for it was much cooler out there.

We went right to bed and fell into a deep troubled sleep for about an hour, then awakened to the grim reality of it all. Though Alfred was exhausted, he was so wonderful and did not ask me not to weep. But we talked and cried, talked and cried. Of course, many and rushing were our regrets. We realized as never before how far off we have been walking from our Savior, and how this has in so many ways lessons to teach us. And we prayed to be willing to be taught.

We were so glad for the dawn of light yesterday morning, and got up at four and cleaned up. Then Alfred and I together went out and were with Kilby quite a long time. He seemed so lovely, his body with the hot weather was still warm. Yet we saw how in just those few days he had grown much thinner. He looked so long when stretched out, and more like a little girl in the Chinese clothes, not our chubby little round Kilby boy. But it was lovely to be able to touch his dear little body one more time, stroke his soft hair, and hold his sweet hands.

Though we called our cook because he loved Kilby so, our cook could not get back as his wife is taking some exam. But my Bible lady could not have been more helpful and like a sister than she was. She talked to me comfortingly, and said so sweetly how she loved Kilby. My dear Chinese sisters began coming early, and much to my surprise encircled me in their arms and shared my tears as you would have done - even though it is not the

Chinese way. So to be only with the Chinese through our sorrow has not been bad at all. They have all become so dear, just as it should be. You were with me, with us, in your prayers though you did not know how much we were needing them.

Our breakfast eating was forced, for it was worse than ever as we sat down with little Kilby's empty high chair in the corner, and my right arm so idle that had cared for him for so many days. After making sure Donny ate enough, we took our song books and Bibles and went to sit again with Kilby. I stroked his little head, cheeks and hair, while Daddy and Donny each held a little foot. There we had our morning family English devotions. We were even able to sing and sang "Asleep in Jesus" and "Have Thine Own Way, Lord." Alfred read I Corinthians 15, and each of us prayed. Then Donny ran out front. When I went to get him, I saw several of our neighbors, so I told them through my tears what had happened.

They were simply stunned as they said, "But he was so well. You kept him so clean and well-fed. How could your baby die? You have such good medicine." And one woman whose baby got well after I gave him some medicine said, "Did not you give your baby the same medicine you gave mine?" I told them all "yes!" These neighbors have heard much of the Gospel, but I have been longing for them to understand more.

Later the women of our street came and with me looked at our precious darling. Of course, they usually do not dress their dead children, but just wrap them in an old cloth. I had such victory as I talked to them and told how we had given him medicine, prayer, and cared for him

– but it was our True God's will to take him to heaven, to that happiest of places. They all agreed he had never known sin (the Chinese are very conscious of sin).

It seemed my tongue was so loose, and I thank God for the love He has given me for the Chinese and for the study of their language. I am beginning to be able to express myself, like I did with these women. But I now see He wished me to know better what the Chinese women have to suffer so often and with so little comfort and no hope. He wishes me to have some tears with my message. I haven't had many tears in my life, but now they come very freely. I begged them to come to the services and to believe. They were touched and tears were in their eyes. One dear lady who thought to be comforting said I could have another baby by the New Year. Yes, it was a good chance to witness to them.

The carpenter came early, and the making of the little coffin in our courtyard did not seem as hard as I thought it would be. We had a lovely little green box made as the Chinese make their coffins, and did not try to have it made in any foreign way. We had several characters painted on each of the long sides, which translated in English are "Christ is the Resurrection" and "Glory Be to God!" At the head, Alfred had a lovely little crown painted, and at the foot, a cross.

We looked at Kilby many more times, but by noon the flies were so bad we had to spray his body with DDT and keep him well-covered. His little lips were turning black, and we could see so many other sign it was just his little dirt shell after all. Of course, with the heat, we knew we must bury him before evening. But it did seem too quick or harsh. We were ready and together lifted his little body into the box, his little head resting on one of his pillows and under his body a little blanket Donny so sweetly brought for him.

Then we were able to sing with our dear Chinese friends without tears as the lid was nailed, and forever from our sight went the little body we had loved, until we see him glorified with Jesus on that Great Day.

After our meal in the afternoon came quite a thunderstorm, so Donny and I sat on Daddy's lap in the parlor and talked of the happy times we would have by God's grace together, and how much more we wanted to love each other and be to each other kinder than ever before.

We committed our darling Donny anew to God, and prayed we will be wise about his future. But how can we keep him from playing with his little Chinese friends if we are to be in the work at all? Others have tried that, and God has still stepped in and claimed His own. Donny is being so wonderful and sweet. He took it so for granted Kilby was now asleep and safe with Jesus, that he was riding in the box to heaven, where he would be very happy playing with Jesus, that he would not come back again, but someday we too would go to heaven to be with him and Jesus.

After the rain, our friends came with two country men who tied ropes across a pole and placed the little box on the ropes and the pole on their shoulders. And then Daddy, Donny, and I went for our last walk by the side of our dear one, followed by many Chinese (though not the women with bound feet). We all wore white,

China's color of mourning.

I kept close to the little coffin, with much of the time my hand resting on the lid. As we passed, the people on the streets seemed so surprised and we heard many remarks: "Yes, that was the foreigners' baby, the one who was so happy and healthy. We saw him riding in his little buggy and on his daddy's bicycle and he never seemed afraid." As I passed groups of women, I would tell them it was my small baby and then my tears could not stay back. They would say, "That's her baby, and her heart is very sad."

It was about two miles to our church's burial grounds, and it seemed God's provision for us to walk in the lovely country air, a blessed outlet for our pent up feelings. As we walked along, we prayed God would help us be more willing to walk the dusty roads of China and to seek souls for Him. We prayed for all the children around us that they, too, might have eternal life.

The dear Christians living near the cemetery met us, and a lovely little grave had already been dug out on the hill near a corn field. The Chinese first dig a grave as we do, then tunnel into the side of the hill and put the coffin inside that cave. We had a wonderful service and Alfred also gave our testimony. Just above the door of the grave cave, Alfred placed a wooded plaque he had carved with "God Is Love" in English and Chinese. And it seemed all was love as Kilby's little coffin was lowered and pushed into the cave out of sight. As I think of it now, I had not even noticed there were no flowers. It was all beautiful without them. But then I was so happy after the earth was mixed with straw and mounded and some little girls placed flowers on top, and their fragrance uplifted us.

Yes, China's soil is a bit more dear now – for out on a little hill, it is receiving back to itself a little heap of dust that was very dear to us. I feel I am nearer to my missionary friends now. For though I had hoped my nurse's training would help me to know more of what to do for my babies, I realize how inadequate it was when God wanted to take my baby to heaven. And I can feel a bit more for them, for now I, too, like so many of them, have a little grave on a hillside in China.

Do pray for me that I shall not allow a questioning attitude to come – for God knows, God cares, and God could have prevented it, but allowed it instead. We feel with the war on we should wait and keep from my becoming pregnant. Then when things are clearer, I already feel such a desire to ask God for another little bundle of love.

We ourselves are taking Chloroidine and Sulfur Dew for several days, hoping there will be no further serious illness among us. And oh, the little snow suit you were sending Kilby with Alfred's sister Abigail, you'd better give it to someone else.

Thank you for typing copies of this letter with carbons as usual, and mailing them to our list. Of course, please send to Alfred's dear family first.

Lovingly,

Your Meggie, Alfred, and dear dear Donny

Rom. 8:28 – "And we know that all things work together for good to those who love God, to those who are the called according to His purpose." What a comfort to us these days to truly believe these words, and to trust our Heavenly Father's marvelous grace will carry us through our loss and grief, and guide our witness to the Chinese in whose midst we live.

PART TWO

1941 to 1950

*"And we know that all things work together
for good to those who love God. . . ."*
Romans 8:28 ~ A favorite verse for many Christians,
including "Meggie" above with "Donny."

Chapter 8

Abbie's Journal
Aug 28, 2003
. . . Romans 8:28 was Mom's life verse for as long as I can remember, and it's mine too. I like to say I inherited it from her. When Phil and I were children, Mom memorized Scripture verses with us to give us strength in times of trouble, maybe even imprisonment for being Christians. Romans 8:28 was one of those verses, along with verses 38 and 39, Ps 1, 23 and 121, Eph 6:10-18, and others. Thankfully, being in prison for my faith or nationality has not been one of my troubles, at least not yet. Sure, I've had my share of tough times, but being able to trust God to work in every situation has always given me hope and peace. I truly can't recall ever feeling depressed or discouraged – weary and sad, yes, and sometimes anxious, but never hopeless or despairing. . .

Shensi Province, China, 1941
Year of Hare

"I'm almost ready," Abigail called to Nathan Jenson, the missionary knocking on her door. "I'll be out in a few minutes. Are all the others there?"

"Yes, the rest of us are loading our bicycles," Nathan said.

His refined baritone voice sent a warm happiness swirling through Abigail *He cares I'm not there yet,* she thought.

She grinned at herself in the small bamboo-framed mirror above the washbasin stand, and smoothed her brown wavy hair, checking the bun in back with her fingers to make sure no pins were loose. She picked up her two saddlebags and bedding roll. A few seconds later, she set them down outside on the cobblestone walk to shut her door, then picked them up again and walked quickly to the central courtyard.

When she reached the bicycle stand, she saw Nathan smiling at her. She smiled back at him, and felt her heartbeat quicken and her cheeks warm.

Elmer Anderson was also smiling at her. To her, he was just another missionary friend, but she was afraid he felt more than friendship for her. And why not! Alfred and Meggie had often talked about her during the year he lived with them before she arrived in China. When the two of them first met several months ago, he had looked at her with hopeful eyes. If it was attraction at first sight for him, it certainly was not for her. These days, the intensity in his eyes made her uncomfortable.

But with Nathan, well, he had stirred up deep feelings within her. Feelings she had not felt before. She remembered Mama saying that about Papa. Now she understood.

If only Mama could see me now, she thought. *Mama would say – Oh min min, my dear daughter. Two fine missionary men attracted to you at the same time. Almost like your Mama long ago. Ja! Be careful, my dear, someone's heart is going to be hurt.*

What a surprise Nathan and Elmer were to Abigail. A year ago she had accepted that God's will for her life might not include a husband. She knew most women who went to the mission field single, stayed single for life, especially nurses like herself dedicated to medicine. There were so few single missionary men, and missionaries were not permitted to marry nationals.

But isn't that how God often works in our lives, she thought, bending over to fasten her bags and bedding roll to her bicycle rack. *Just when we think we're giving up something for the Kingdom, God surprises us and gives it back.*

"My bicycle is all loaded and ready to go," Nathan said, walking over to her side. "It looks like you're ready too."

*   *   *

To reach what they called Mount Jubilee, the small group of missionaries Abigail and Nathan were traveling with endured six days of bicycling on dusty, dirty roads and pushing their bikes up steep rocky trails. But the hardships seemed like nothing as they joyfully anticipated their mission's annual conference. How wonderful it would be to worship in English and Swedish, and to fellowship with other missionaries and hear news from abroad.

By the end of the second day of bicycling, Abigail and Nathan were an obvious couple. They rode together, ate together, talked and sang together. Each evening when they stopped for the night at an inn or temple, her brown head and his red one could be seen close together in the light of a lantern reading the Bible or praying or softly talking.

Although it was too early to speak of marriage,

they felt in their hearts they had found their life's partner. And they radiated this joy to everyone around them, even to the throngs of Chinese who crowded close whenever they stopped.

In one village they heard a man say, "Look, she must be his concubine. See how they gaze at each other and touch." Then the crowd laughed loudly as though at a huge joke. When Abigail tried to correct the mistaken impression, the onlookers laughed even harder, mocking her discomfort.

"Fine missionaries we are if they think that," Nathan said with a grin. "We'll have to be more circumspect."

Abigail nodded. "I won't look at you if you won't look at me."

At that, they both burst into laughter at themselves. The oldest missionary among them, a single lady, looked at them and frowned. She refrained from saying anything. But for the rest of the trip, she was their self-appointed chaperone, even when they stopped to sit side by side and dangle their tired feet in a clear stream on the last afternoon.

*   *   *

The mission conference in the cool, comfortable summer cottages of Mount Jubilee was a time when life-long friendships were made, much like the to-the-death friendships of those who serve together in the military. The sorrowing were comforted, the discouraged were encouraged, the lonely were befriended, joys were celebrated, and children were adored, especially the new babies.

It was also a time for new missionaries to share

their testimonies. Nathan shared his during the service the second evening. As he started to speak, his tall handsomeness and pleasing voice immediately caught everyone's attention.

"I grew up on a Swedish farm in Minnesota," he began. "So I can give my testimony in Swedish or English." Everyone smiled. Then he added, "Just don't ask me to do it in Mandarin yet." And everyone laughed.

"I was one of seven sons and three daughters. But there was always enough love and food for everyone. One day when I was out doing farm chores with my father, he startled me by saying, 'Son, I don't think you're cut out to be a farmer. I think you should consider teaching.'

"I was thrilled at his words because I loved books. So even though the others in my family did not, I finished high school and then went to normal school for a year. I remember it as one of the richest experiences in my life.

"During my school years, many preachers and missionaries stayed in our home. My mother was a wonderful cook and a generous hostess who loved to entertain God's servants. Once we hosted a missionary couple from China who spoke so powerfully to us. That evening I truly gave my life to Christ. Not long after, I heard another missionary from China speak on the radio. Her name was Mrs. Charles Cowman."

Nathan's listeners nodded and smiled when they heard her beloved name.

"At the time I heard Mrs. Cowman, I had already been teaching in a country school for two years.

As much as I liked teaching, I decided to attend Moody Bible Institute in Chicago to prepare for missionary service. My family fully supported me in every way, praise God!

"While I was at Moody, several men from our mission visited me and impressed me with the need for missionaries in China. You can see the result. Here I am. But as you know, it was extremely difficult and dangerous to get here. Although I arrived in Shanghai two years ago, I was stuck there because of the fighting and bombing. However, God turned my waiting time into useful language study.

"At last, along with these others," he named and gestured to them, "I did the French Indo-China route to you here in Free China. God willing, that's a six-month journey I hope never to do again. We traveled by boat, train, mule cart, old trucks, and of course, by bicycle and our own legs. Several times, we were nearly captured by soldiers. And I'm sure we escaped death many more times than we knew. I wish I could be there when my father who thought I wasn't cut out for farm life reads some of my letters."

He chuckled, and his listeners joined him.

"But thanks be to God, here I am to do His will. And I'm so glad to meet many of you whose names I've heard or read."

As he ended his testimony, his eyes met Abigail's. There was a pause as the others watched, wondering. Then someone started a song and he sat down. Soon dozens of voices were singing in harmony and with joy as only missionaries can sing:

He leadeth me, O blessed thought!
O words with heavenly comfort fraught!
Whate'er I do, where'er I be,
Still 'tis God's hand that leadeth me.

During the next morning's business session, Nathan was elected mission secretary, a great honor and a great responsibility. Because he confessed to being a poor typist, Abigail was elected his assistant. Each evening after the services, they worked together in the general meeting room to prepare the daily business minutes for the next day. The other missionaries soon considered them a perfect couple. Many knowing smiles and nods were exchanged when Abigail and Nathan weren't looking, and a few even when they were.

* * *

Abbie's Journal
Sep 7, 2003

. . . recently I read a new biography about Gladys Aylward and the hundreds of Chinese orphans she rescued during that time of war by marching them many miles to safety. As in many of the books and movies about her, there was a mystery somebody in white who nursed Miss Aylward back to life and health when she nearly died after that long march. Lots of people have speculated about who the "angel in white" was. I know well who the "angel" was. She was my Aunt Abigail who was living with my family at their mission station where Miss A collapsed. I grew up hearing Miss A stories from Auntie herself, and also from Dad and Mom who were a bit ticked that Miss A always spoke as if real angels helped her instead of other missionaries, such as Aunt Abigail and themselves. I also heard how she and a Chinese

army officer were in love and wanted to marry. But that was taboo for missionaries back then, so she didn't. . .

. . . after caring for Miss Aylward, Auntie became nurse for Donny while Mom was pregnant with me and bedfast. Sadly, the bombings and deprivations of war were just too much for his sick seven-year old body. At his death, how Auntie must have wept with my parents – and not just for him, but also for little Kilby whose grave was still new. What a comfort it must have been for her soon afterwards to have the joy of her engagement and marriage to Uncle Nathan, and the birth of her namesake, baby me. . .

Chapter 9

Abbie's Journal
Sep 19, 2003
. . . my fondest memory of Aunt Abigail is of her chatting with Mom, their young children playing happily around them. They had thirteen children between them – so they had lots to laugh about, but also lots to cry about. For they raised their children in China during the dreadful war years of the 30s and 40s – and sadly, five died. In addition to caring for their own families and friends, as missionary nurses they also did evangelism and medical work in a country at war whose people were desperate for help. . .

Sian, China, 1942
Year of Horse

At the mission center's blacked out window, Alfred stood listening, his body tense. He couldn't see them, but he could hear countless people rushing about, shouting and sobbing, looking for refuge. The air raid sirens had begun their piercing wails several minutes ago, so he knew the public bomb shelters were already crammed beyond capacity.

Across the room, Meggie lay resting on the bed, sweet little Abbie asleep in her arms. The approaching bombers did not seem to disturb them.

After the first siren blast a few minutes earlier, Abigail had run into the room. Meggie had raised her head and said yet again, "No, dear, we're not going to

104

the bomb shelter this time. God can protect us here. And if he chooses not to, then soon we'll be with dear Donny and Kilby in heaven. You hurry and go with Nathan."

Abigail had quickly kissed her new namesake's tiny soft cheek and run to Nathan waiting at the door. Alfred was glad his sister no longer pled with them to seek safety. He wanted to, but Meggie insisted she wasn't recovered enough to go back and forth from their room to the bomb shelter. Besides, she had told him between sobs, she wanted to avoid what had happened to their beloved Donny.

As Alfred moved to the other blackened window, he prayed silently. *Almighty God, help us to know you are with us. Help me to be as trusting as Meggie. Please protect our sweet little Abbie. And thank you, oh thank you for not leaving us with empty arms. We praise you for the assurance Donny and Kilby are now safe in your arms forever.*

At that moment, a flower-like fragrance unexpectedly drifted over to him from where Meggie and baby Abbie lay. He looked upwards and murmured again, *Thank you, oh thank you.*

Slowly his shoulders relaxed. And though the drone of the Japanese bombers had become a deafening roar, he tiptoed over to the bed. Lying down on his side facing Meggie, he stretched his arm protectingly over his family. His heart was at peace, but his mind jolted back to the day Donny died.

*   *   *

Donny had been convulsing when Alfred rushed him to the Sian Christian Hospital, where the British missionary doctor was swift with her diagnosis.

"I'm quite sure it's the severest strain of meningitis," Dr. Jenkins had said. "That means your son's only chance of surviving is twenty-four hour care. We must respond to every change immediately. Donny should not be left alone even for a minute. "

She shook her head sadly. "If it weren't for this war, we would have better medicines for him." Then she laid her hands on Donny's head and urgently prayed for God's will, and for grace and strength for each of them.

Because Meggie was bedfast during the final months of her third pregnancy, a difficult one this time, Abigail quickly agreed to be her nephew's full-time nurse. Alfred and Nathan took turns giving her breaks every few hours. They also took turns being with Meggie and little Abbie.

It was an extremely anxious time, made even more so by frequent bombings and bombing scares. Nearly every day, they heard the air raid sirens and the frightening drone of Japanese bombers. Each time, they carefully rushed Donny to one of the hospital's bomb shelters, and Meggie and the baby to the mission station one.

In spite of being frequently moved when he should have been kept still, Donny seemed to improve every day. Meggie, who hadn't seen him for weeks, wept with joy the day she heard he could soon leave the hospital.

The day of Donny's release, Alfred brought him a new outfit of clothes to wear – a gift from Chinese Christians who were praying for their little friend. While he and Abigail were dressing him, sirens suddenly broke into their happy mood. Alfred quickly picked up Donny and hurried to the shelter. Abigail followed with what things she could hastily collect.

They crouched together in the shelter with Donny across their laps. He held tightly to their hands as the bombers flew low overhead. They held their breaths, but the planes passed without dropping any bombs.

When they could no longer hear the planes, Donny smiled up at Alfred and said, "Daddy, God kept us safe again, didn't He? Tell Mommy we're safe." He closed his eyes, and his little body slowly became limp.

Stunned and disbelieving, Alfred and Abigail looked at each other and wept. They gently shook Donny and rubbed his little body. Dr. Jenkins saw what was happening and rushed from the other end of the shelter to be with them.

"Oh no!" she said. "How I prayed this wouldn't happen! But I was afraid God might take your Donny. I was afraid all the moving back and forth might be too much for his weakened heart. I'm so sorry, so very, very sorry." She encircled them with her arms, and others in the shelter crowded close to comfort and pray.

As soon as the all-clear siren blew, Alfred and Abigail together carried Donny to Meggie's room several blocks away. Dr Jenkins was concerned Meggie would collapse, so she went with them. Instead, Meggie got out of bed and insisted on rocking Donny and telling him goodbye.

After a while, Alfred and Nathan went to help a carpenter hastily make Donny's small coffin. Abigail and Dr. Jenkins stayed with Meggie and Donny and little Abbie.

Several hours later, Donny's open coffin was placed in front of the pulpit in the mission church. Word of his death spread quickly, and hundreds of Chinese and a number of missionaries gathered for his funeral, and to support Alfred and Meggie and Abigail.

So that little Donny could be buried before dark in the Christian Cemetery, his service was held in the afternoon. In Chinese and then in English, the congregation sang Meggie's favorite hymn, Blessed Assurance Jesus Is Mine, as well as Alfred's, Nearer My God to Thee.

By the time Alfred shared a few words, everyone was weeping with him and Meggie. Their tears were not just from sorrow, but also from the powerful sense of God's holy presence there with all of them.

"Some of you may feel sorry for us and say that God has now taken our second beloved son and left us with a baby daughter," Alfred said. "But instead I say, see how God has not left us with empty arms. He has given us a precious little girl to make us smile again."

With tears streaming down his face, he gazed down at little Abbie sleeping peacefully in his arms.

"Look how our heavenly Father has given us a daughter to love and care for, and to remind everyone here that females are just as important to God as males." He paused to let his hearers think about his words, then continued. "God comforts Meggie and me with the assurance our young sons – and many of your loved ones too – are now forever safe in the arms of Jesus. Never again will our loved ones experience sorrow or suffering. And someday, we will all be joyfully reunited in heaven.

"Yes! The Holy Book teaches us how Jesus can change the black dragons that come into our lives to red dragons of blessings when we give our lives to True God. Glory be to God!"

At the end of the funeral, dozens of Chinese came forward to the altar to pray to True God *Zhen Shen* for the first time in their lives.

*   *   *

A week later, Meggie and Alfred asked Abigail and Nathan to go with them to Donny's grave. They wanted to do what they had not been able to do right after the burial– cover the raw earth with flowers. On their way to the cemetery, their rickshaws stopped at the market place, where they bought two large baskets of fragrant spring blossoms.

Walking to Donny's grave from the cemetery gate, Meggie sensed the others were just as exhausted as she was and as fearful of sirens sounding. But after they knelt by the flower-covered grave and Nathan prayed aloud, she looked into their faces and saw they too, like she, felt comforted and renewed.

As they prepared to walk back to the waiting rickshaws, Abigail said, "Stop, please. I have something important to share with you. And now is the best time and place. I must tell you what happened to me this morning."

The others stopped abruptly and looked intently at her.

"I was awakened early this morning by a feeling of amazing calm spreading over me," she said. "I've never felt anything like it before. I sat up in my bed and saw a gleaming light filling the corner of my room. It was the brightest, loveliest light I've ever seen. And it wasn't sunlight, for outside was still dark.

"While I stared in wonder, I heard or maybe felt an unfamiliar voice say, 'Don't be afraid! Everything will be all right!' After the light and soothing words faded away, I somehow knew God wanted me to give you this message. Dear Alfred and Abbie, your darling Abbie will not die young. She will live a long life committed to God, and so will another child yet to be born."

No one moved or said anything. After a time, Meggie walked slowly away from Donny's grave. She cradled little Abbie in one arm and put her other arm through one of Alfred's. They walked silently to the cemetery gate. Abigail and Nathan followed, hand in hand.

As Alfred helped Meggie into her waiting rickshaw, she could still smell the fragrance of the flowers they had lovingly placed on Donny's grave. Through her tears, she smiled down at little Abbie, patted Alfred's arm, then said to the coolie, "*Ching hui jah bah.* Let us go home, please."

The three other rickshaws followed hers back to the mission station.

*   *   *

Abbie's Journal
Sep 29, 2003

. . . *from my youngest days, I knew there was something extra special between Aunt Abigail and my family. Wasn't I her namesake niece? Didn't she always have a special hug and smile for me? The youngest child, Auntie was born two years after Dad's sister Hilda was brutally murdered by angry Chinese rioters. Martyred, my family always says. So Auntie seemed like a gift from God to her family – a promise of hope in a dark, dangerous time. Like Auntie before me, I too was a precious child, surrounded by my parents' love and hers, and by the kindnesses of many others, both Chinese and Westerners. And like her, I lived like a child princess in the land of my birth – chaotic China – unaware until I was older that bombings and devastation and nasty deaths and fleeing aren't normal, everyday life. . .*

Chapter 10

A letter home from Meggie
Kien-yang, near Sian, China, 1942
Year of Horse

August 2, 1942
My own dearest Mother and Dad and Mother Ruth (carbon copy),

How wonderful to receive TWO letters from you this week! We have read them over and over, and feel greatly comforted. But oh, how difficult to accept that now you will not meet our two darling sons until heaven. Do not fear that our faith is shaken. Rather, it is strengthened! God knows what is best for the Kingdom, and He has not left us with empty arms. You would be so delighted with our darling little Abbie, as are we. Even though she cannot understand, I tell her stories about the good times her brothers are having with Jesus. But of course, I still weep every day for our unspeakable loss, even as I see that our love for her is a great witness to the Chinese around us about the value of a girl child.

As you say, what a marvelous difference the new airplane mail service makes – these recent letters from you took only six weeks to reach us, and most of that time was travel here in China. I always marvel when your letters even reach us, considering all the fighting going on. Yes, we are in Free China, as this part of the country is called these days, but we are surrounded by war zones.

Enough said on that – perhaps even those few words will be blacked out by censors.

You asked for a story from China to share this Christmas in church and in a carbon letter to our supporters. Here is one. Alfred assures me I have told it carefully enough not to endanger anyone. . .

Grandma Han's Christmas Message

It wasn't even light when Grandma Han awakened that morning. She slid quietly off her kang bed to allow her precious grandsons to sleep as late as possible.

First, she wrapped her feet that had been unbound in strips of cloth – not tightly, but tight enough so that her feet would have strength for the walk to the factory. Next, she lit her little charcoal stove after taking it outside of her one-room home. It was the room billeted to them when they had arrived as a happy family of five several years ago. But that happiness was short-lived, for a new army had taken control of the area – Mao Tse-tung's army. When the Communists arrived, they promised they would not even borrow a needle from Grandma Han. But then instead, they had taken her son and her daughter-in-law. At least, the new soldiers were still allowing her to care for her two grandsons.

No more time for reflecting this hour of the day – the rice must be boiled, peanuts and soybeans toasted, and vegetables with a bit of pepper and meat fried in readiness for quick departures. The boys were now up and dressed neatly in their school uniforms, and out the door as soon as Grandma handed them their food buckets for their morning and noon rice meals. Each boy grabbed his bucket and went bounding down the street. Childhood held no fears as yet for these children – even under Communism.

Evening came. Grandma Han had worked hard all day at the factory. As she limped home, she felt fortunate the factory where she was assigned was close to her little one-room home in the large barracks. Years before in her childhood, her father had insisted that her feet be bound to please her future husband. Now though her feet were unbound, her deformed arches and toes would always cripple and pain her, and cause her to limp when she walked.

Her two precious grandsons were already home. Soon they were eating warmed up soupy rice with leftovers from the morning's peanuts and vegetables, and telling her about their school day and street sweeping. For a special treat to celebrate the day, she had gotten them each a banana, which they were enjoying with appreciative smacking.

Suddenly, there was a loud knock on the door. Her heart went cold with dread. She had heard that same forceful commanding sound when the Commies had forced her son and then her daughter-in-law to join their "liberating" army. Quickly, she tucked her grandsons under their quilt. Perhaps the one dim candle would not reveal their hideout. She opened the door. Two soldiers rushed in.

"What are you doing, old grandma?" one

demanded. "Did you work well and productively today at the factory?"

"Ah, yes, yes!" she said, bowing. And indeed she had.

She was not surprised when the soldiers grabbed her worn little Bible from the center of her small bamboo table. They jeered at the Bible, then tore it into pieces and threw them into a far corner of the room. She regretted she had taken it earlier from its hiding place. "Go to bed immediately!" one of the large soldiers yelled. "And see to it you are well-rested and at the factory earlier than usual tomorrow morning!"

They stomped out of the room, scarcely looking at the rumpled old quilt on the kang bed.

Ah! Thanks be to Zhen Shen True God, the soldiers were gone!

Grandma Han crept on her knees over to where her Holy Bible was scattered. She held her candle close and began to read in a soft voice from one of the pieces the words of Jesus, "Let not your heart be troubled. Ye believe in God, believe also in me. . ."

For a long while, she knelt there. Then gently, she wrapped the precious fragments of her Bible in a cloth, and hid the bundle in its secret place. After blowing out the candle, she lay down under the quilt between her grandsons.

"Duo shieh, chin ai-de Yeh-Su! Thank you, dearest Jesus!" she murmured in prayer as she stroked her grandsons' cheeks. "Thank you for protecting us on this your special day - the day you were born!"

The young boys were soon asleep. But Grandma Han lay awake for a long time, her soul comforted and warmed by remembered carols singing in her heart.

Yes, dear far away family, like Grandma Han, our hearts are warmed by Jesus' promises in God's Word and in the carols and hymns we sing. God knows how much we need that comfort and healing these days. You urge us to return home to America before we are all gone. Be assured, we will do so as God leads the way. For surely, oh surely, God will let you hold in your arms at least one of your China-born grandchildren.

Because I must be careful what I say, I close now.

Lovingly,

Your Meggie, Alfred, and our dear dear little Abbie

PS – I have no instrument to play these days because of course we couldn't bring along our small organ or accordion when we fled. So when I feel extra sad or afraid, I sing or mediate on the words of "Be not dismayed whate're betide. God will take care of you." When your worries for us become too a great burden, sing with me, and God will carry our burdens together.

Chapter 11

Abbie's Journal
Feb 26, 2004

. . .Phil's birthday is today. He's a real American, like Mom, born in America when I was four. When I phoned him to wish him Happy Birthday, I called him "little Marine," his nickname as a baby because he was born while Dad was serving in intelligence with the Marines in China during WWII. After we chatted a bit about Dad's secret intelligence work, Phil reminded me he has no memories of his own of China, just what he's heard and seen in photos. I find that strange because I have many memories from when I was three and four.

. . . Phil doesn't even remember Chengtu when he and Web, one of his lifelong buddies, first played together where our families were living under compound arrest. I still remember how they squabbled over his tricycle until Mom told Web's dad to somehow get Web his own. We sure didn't guess back then that years later, as high school seniors, they would bicycle completely around Taiwan. Phil agrees with me that he was more traumatized by our escape from China than we all realized at the time, and that trauma affected his China memories. I know the trauma gave me decades of war nightmares. . .

Shanghai, "City of Refuge," China, 1948
Year of Rat

The day after Alfred was discharged from the U.S. military, he mailed his Marine Corps uniforms and other sensitive items to his brother Oliver in the States. He would have mailed the bulky APO package to Meggie, but she was already en route by ship to China, returning with Abbie and little Philly from the States. The three of them had enjoyed living safely with relatives while Alfred, with his fluent Mandarin, served in China as an interpreter for intelligence during the final years of World War II. That he had agreed to continue in intelligence as he resumed his missionary life, no one could know, not even Meggie.

Thinking how relieved he was to back to his regular life, Alfred hummed to himself as he stepped off the train onto the Shanghai station platform. He looked around quickly to see if anyone had come to meet him. Not seeing anyone he recognized in the crowd, he hurried with his briefcase and suitcase to the exit gates. As he walked through one of the gates, he heard a familiar voice call his name.

Alfred looked to his right and called back, "Nathan! How wonderful of you to meet me! I wasn't sure if my cablegram would reach the mission center before me." He set his suitcase down and stretched out his hand to his brother-in-law.

"How's the retired Captain?" Nathan said, clasping Alfred's hand. "Say, it's good to see you looking like a civilian again."

Nathan picked up Alfred's suitcase, and the two men strode to the rickshaw stand.

The evening meal had already begun when they reached the mission center. The tables were full because missionaries from all over China were leaving the country due to the escalation of the civil war between

Chiang's Nationalists and Mao's Communists. The mission hostess added places for the two men at the table where Abigail and her children were seated. Many hearty words of welcome greeted the men as they sat down.

The dining room quieted while Alfred and Nathan bowed their heads in silent prayer. But as soon as they lifted their heads, animated discussion continued at the others tables. Alfred quickly learned about a serious problem. Four tons of Chinese Scriptures from the Bible Society were waiting in a warehouse for delivery to the Sian area where they had been requested months ago. Due to the civil war, the usual train and river routes were blocked. So how could these Bibles get to their destination in these devastating times? That was the problem needing a speedy solution, even though it seemed there was none.

"What do you think, Alfred?" the mission director asked. "You've traveled to Sian from here more than the rest of us. How can we get these Bibles to Sian in the event the fighting shuts down all transportation?"

"What about the new motor roads between here and there?" Alfred asked. "I haven't heard anyone mention them this evening. I've driven many miles on them for my Marine Corps assignments. Sure, only a few stretches of pavement are finished, but the dirt and gravel roadbeds are passable. I think you should consider driving the Bibles to Sian."

"But we don't have any trucks," the director replied.

Alfred nodded his head. "True, but I have an idea," he said.

In the momentary silence, he sensed all eyes on him. He knew he had a reputation as a clever problem solver. But could he solve this situation that seemed impossible?

Alfred looked up at the ceiling and squinted. He pushed his glasses up a bit on his nose. "I think I know what to do," he said. "There's a good chance I can secure a few U.S. military trucks and jeeps since America pretty much abandoned all its equipment when the military pulled out. I'll see what I can arrange first thing tomorrow."

The director looked around the room. "If Alfred succeeds, who is willing to go on this trip, this Bible convoy? We'll need drivers and helpers."

He walked over to Alfred and laid his hand on Alfred's shoulder. "Would you be willing to lead the Bible convoy?" he asked.

"Perhaps! Actually, I'd be thrilled to! But as you know, Meggie and the children are arriving here in a few weeks, and my main purpose in coming here is to meet them. However, if Nathan will agree to join the convoy, then I suppose my dear sister," he smiled over at Abigail, "won't mind waiting here with her young ones to welcome Meggie. But for tonight, I suggest we postpone any more planning until we see what vehicles God provides."

"Then let's move to the parlor for our evening prayers and tea," the director said. "Those of you with wee ones, please feel free to retire to your rooms."

"And I think I'll retire, too," Alfred said. "I've

some unexpected praying and preparing to do, so please excuse me." He picked up his briefcase and suitcase in the front hall, and followed the hostess to a guestroom.

The next morning, when Nathan and Abigail entered the dining room for breakfast with their children, they looked around for Alfred.

The hostess noticed them and said, "If you're looking for your brother, he grabbed an early bite in the kitchen and left about an hour ago for the U.S. military warehouses. His eyes were sparkling, so I have a good feeling about his plans. But he didn't tell me anything or leave a message for you."

*   *   *

A week later, on February 16, five decommissioned U.S. military vehicles, three trucks and two jeeps with trailers, formed a line at sunrise in front of the Shanghai Mission Center on Sinza Lu Street. Thanks to many miracles, the Bible convoy to Sian was loaded and ready to depart. Alfred, Nathan, and three new missionary men were the drivers. Accompanying them were two women, the wife of one of the men and a single lady missionary. In addition, the Nationalist government had provided two armed guards for each vehicle along with the government's protection flags now flying from each vehicle.

Repeatedly quizzed about how he had managed to arrange all this, Alfred just shrugged and said, "God used my Marine Corps ties for His Kingdom's work."

At 7:16, Alfred's piercing, two-fingers-in-the-mouth whistle caught everyone's attention. "Are we ready to roll?" he called from beside the lead jeep that he was driving. "Then it's time to get moving. But first, we'll commit this convoy to God as we do all our voyages."

The convoy members moved to stand beside the mission director. The large group of missionaries and Chinese Christians who had gathered to bid them God-speed circled around the departing missionaries and the vehicles. Beyond them stood the guards, ensuring that a rapidly growing crowd of curious Chinese spectators kept their distance.

As soon as the director said "Amen," Abigail, with tears rolling down her cheeks, started their familiar farewell song:

> God be with you til we meet again;
> By His counsels guide, uphold you,
> With His sheep securely fold you;
> God be with you til we meet again.
> God be with you til we meet again.

By the end of the first verse, five motors were running and all convoy members and guards were in their seats. By the end of the second verse, the Bible convoy was moving slowly down the street. As Alfred turned off Sinza Lu, the view in his rearview mirror was the four vehicles behind him and behind them dozens of waving white hankies. He waved his arm one last time from the jeep and beeped his horn. One by one, the other drivers followed his example, and the women wiped tears from their cheeks.

That evening, with only the discomfort of rain and muddy roads most of the day, the Bible convoy reached its destination goal – the mission home of the Englunds in Hangchow. The new missionaries were alert and fascinated as they drove through this historic city, the first headquarters of Dr. Hudson Taylor's missionary work, established in 1865.

The Englunds shared some of the stories they'd heard about the "old days" during the simple but tasty supper of soup and onion flat breads. The guards ate their meal squatting in the mission courtyard. The missionaries ate inside at the dining table, and talked about the Bible convoy and speculated on the risks ahead of them in these uncertain times of war.

They would all have liked to share and pray long into the night. But since the convoy needed to leave at sunrise the next day, an early bedtime took precedence. While the men and guards slept in their bed-bags in the vehicles, the two women enjoyed the luxury and security of the Englunds' guestroom.

Just before the women fell asleep, Phyllis said to the new missionary wife, "Better enjoy this, Carol, we won't have many more nights this comfortable, in fact, maybe not anymore."

*   *   *

Abbie's Journal
Mar 19, 2004
. . . I never know what I'm going to "discover" when I look through Dad's photo collection. I'm reading a little book about his final Bible convoy in China in 1948. And lo and behold (one of Dad's expressions), I just now found his photo of the book's author. A fun, God-directed coincidence. . .

Phyllis, the Bible Convoy journaler.

Chapter 12

Abbie's Journal
Mar 20, 2004

. . . *after I finished the Bible convoy book yesterday, I did some online Googling for the author, Phyllis Taylor. The folks kept in contact with her for many years. But during their final illnesses and then deaths, our family lost contact with her. I still remember her from when I was a little girl in China and called her "Auntie" Phyllis. She was one of the fun single missionaries (not all of them were fun), and from England.*

. . . *unfortunately, my renewed interest in Phyllis is too late. She's already joined the folks in heaven, along with many other China missionaries who made my younger days happy and secure in spite of the horrors of war all around us. I did find out Phyllis had several more missionary books published, most of them no longer available. But I just ordered her latest book online from Amazon titled,* China: The Reluctant Exodus, *published in 2000. I'm eager for it to arrive. . .*

Bible Convoy from Shanghai to Sian, China, 1948
Same Year of Rat

Phyllis Thompson, the single woman missionary on the Bible convoy, soon assumed the role as the convoy's journaler. She preferred riding in the lead jeep with Fred, so she could hear from him first hand where they were and what was going on. Every time the convoy stopped for meals or vehicle breakdowns or swollen river ferries, she pulled out her black notebook and jotted down the latest events.

After their evening meal, she often read to the others from her journal. Sometimes the entries were just brief descriptions of their travels that day, for nothing too much out of the ordinary had happened. However, more often her entries were cleverly told stories of adventure or danger. On the evening of February 26, she read aloud by candlelight to her exhausted missionary companions:

>Early this morning it started to rain, a steady, penetrating drizzle which continued all day. The men bundled their bed-bags into the trucks, and went to see what were the prospects of getting across the river. The Tunglu River was rather wide at this point, and although the ferry boat was large enough to take two vehicles at a time, it was evident that it would be a matter of two or three hours before our vehicles could all get over.

>The driver of the empty bus we had spent the night in and were still occupying came along and looked rather surprised to find us there! When we thanked him for the use of it, however, he was quite affable. He would not be crossing the river today, he said, as the roads were too muddy to proceed, so we were welcome to remain in his bus.

>Fortunately, the ferry was working. We had feared lest the river should be too high.

There was only one vehicle ahead of our five to cross over, so the rear jeep was taken over in the first ferry load. It was a tricky ferry to mount. The roadway was built up right into the river bed, for sometimes the waters were very low. The ferry boat, therefore, was unable to come within about thirty feet of the water's edge, and the vehicles had to drive on to it by way of two narrow gangways with joins in the middle, producing a hinge-like narrow effect. As the jeep trailers often manifested a tendency to independent action and swerved disconcertingly when they encountered bumps in the road, it was a relief when the jeep and trailer had safely negotiated the hinge, and landed with a bump on the boat. The ferry was poled slowly across the river, and returned in about half an hour for our next two vehicles.

What moments! Alfred, clad from neck to ankles in a khaki-coloured airman's suit, his curly hair uncovered, got into his jeep, while Nathan climbed into the driver's seat of his truck. The jeep engine stated, and slowly the pugnacious little machine chugged down the muddy road, and nosed its two front wheels on to the gangways. Chinese line the banks, silently watching. Coolies shout and the ferrymen press their long poles deeper into the water, holding the barge-like ferry steady as the jeep with its trailer moved slowly up the gangways. They bend dangerously at that hinge-like join, but the trailer came up straight. Bump, bump, and the jeep was over the ridge where the gangway ended, and slid slowly into the middle of the ferry. The jeep was safe! Fred remained at the wheel, ready to move slowly forward to balance the barge as our first heavy truck came on board.

And now for the truck, laden with Bibles. Gordon sat at the wheel in his white, roll-collar sweater, his eyes fixed on the ferry boat. He's only been in China about three weeks – how strange everything must seem! He saw the ferrymen gesticulating, waving him on, and shouting. Slowly the truck slipped down the road and the front wheels crawled on to the gangways. The mudguards and hood blocked Gordon's line of vision, and could not see the gangways – only those gesticulating ferrymen. They waved him on, and slowly he eased up the clutch. The back wheels were stopped against the gangways, and as he accelerated, they came up on to them with a jerk. Up the truck went, over that join which bent sharply under the weight. But for a moment it was all right! The front wheels were almost at the barge!

And then something happened. One of the outside planks had snapped. The truck seemed to stop, veer over to one side, hover for an awful moment in the air, and then reeled slowly over, down into the river.

I stood watching helplessly, unable to move. There was shouting, coolies ran about, and then Nathan dashed past me, right down into the water.

Phyllis stopped reading and looked over at Nathan.

He said, "I suppose you thought I'd lost my head. But all I could think of was getting to Gordon. I didn't think of anything else. I was so afraid for Gordon."

But Gordon was safe. Even before Nathan had reached the truck, Gordon pushed the truck's door open and upwards, and crawled out. One of the Chinese on the ferry had helped him down from the capsized truck and onto the ferry.

"I learned some new Mandarin vocabulary today," Nathan said, "and not from a textbooks." The others chuckled with him.

And so began a harried, week-long delay for the convoy, beginning with the immediate recovery of the truck's endangered contents, especially the cases of Bibles, metal containers of medicines, and drums of gasoline.

As soon as the truck was empty, Alfred supervised getting it back onto its wheels. He hooked a pulley to a tree and ran a stout rope through it. One end of the rope he fastened to the capsized truck and the other to Nathan's truck. Once righted and back on shore, the truck started up as if nothing had happened. Its next attempt on to the ferry was successful. By nightfall, it and the other vehicles had been safely ferried across the river.

In relief and gratitude, the seven wet, muddy and weary missionaries sang together the Doxology. The crowd who had been watching for hours were so surprised and amused that they burst into loud laughter and cheers for the foreign devils. But they quickly quieted when Alfred shared with them in his fluent Chinese why he and the others had just sung to God, *Zhen Shen* True God.

To their dismay, several cases of Bibles were soaked. Because drizzling rain kept the sunshine away for days, the Bibles were carefully spread out and dried inside a rented room and covered porch in a nearby village. While the Bibles and other items dried, the missionaries took turns doing what missionaries do. They held evening street meetings with singing and preaching, passed out tracts in the morning markets, and tended to the sick and injured in afternoon clinics.

*   *   *

Days later, when the Bible convoy was back on the road again, driving along at its usual rate of fifteen to twenty miles an hour, Alfred said to Phyllis, "Isn't it amazing how God's hand is always present, even in accidents like the truck's tipping over?"

"But I prefer it when God keeps the accidents from happening," Phyllis said.

"If our truck hadn't capsized into the river, we never would have stayed in that village," Alfred answered. "And now there are new Christians there and hopefully the start of a Gospel Hall. Praise Almighty God!"

"I agree," Phyllis said. "But we also have hundreds of damaged Bibles, and what if Gordon had been hurt or killed or some of the rest of us?"

"It's a battle for God's Kingdom we're waging," Alfred replied thoughtfully. "Battles have casualties, even when they're won."

"Of course, my mind knows that. But my heart sometimes has a hard time accepting it as trustingly as you seem to" Phyllis said.

Neither of them mentioned Alfred's two young sons buried in the city where they were headed. But neither did they speak for several minutes.

Then Phyllis said, "You know what I've decided to do? I've been thinking about it for several days now since the accident. I'm going to turn my convoy journal into a book. Christians in England and America need to hear about the battles, as you call them, that we face over here alongside our Chinese brothers and sisters. I want to write something more lasting than articles, although they're important, too, of course."

"I hope you'll do it, Phyllis! Too many of us have good intentions about writing books and then never finish for one reason or another. And yes, indeed, our Bible convoy is turning out to be an extraordinary story, one to encourage faith."

Several evenings later, before she read aloud from her journal, Phyllis told the others about her hopes of turning her journal into a book. They assured her they'd be praying for her, and asked her to be sure they each got several copies.

"That is if we make it to Sian alive," the one wife in the group said. A new missionary, she had already shared several times that she had had no real understanding until this convoy experience of what "roughing it" or "living simply" meant. "Like those boat-dwellers yesterday on the river who served us dinner in their boat. Did you write about them, Phyllis?"

"I did. Here's what I have so far. Listen, everyone."

The junk was about thirty-five feet from bow to stern, and seven feet at the beam. The cabins cannot be more than twelve feet long and six feet wide, and yet in these small spaces families live. We were amazed at the cleanliness and tidiness we found in the small cabin we entered. It was divided into two small compartments, with wide ledges on either side, which are used as beds during the nights and for seats during the day. The wood work was of light wood, well polished and clean, and the curved roof was brown and shiny. Beyond us in the small kitchen area in the open were two women and a baby. An oblong chest served as a table in the middle of the cabin, and we sat on either side of it. The orthodox number of four plates of vegetables was placed in the middle of the table, and our bowls of steamed rice were handed to us from the kitchen area. It was all so simple, and to be suddenly called upon to provide a meal for extra people seemed to present no difficulty to the calm and cheerful little boatwomen.

The boat-dwellers of China! In junks and barges, millions of them move along the rivers and canals, here to-day and gone tomorrow.

Their mobile existence makes them difficult to reach with the Gospel, for consecutive work amongst them is almost impossible. There have been missionaries who have been so burdened for them that they themselves have lived on boats, in order to better reach these simple people.

"Like my parents did years ago," Alfred murmured, interrupting, and the others nodded. "But do go ahead, read some more. I'd like to hear what you wrote about the Lantern Festival. That was a bit scary, wasn't it?"

"I'll say so," Nathan said. "I knew you were right, Alfred. We had to get out of there, even though we were already set up for the night. That dragon – I believe it was rushing back and forth because we were there. We were upsetting the atmosphere, like Jesus and the demons in the Gospels. Yes, who knows what that crowd might have done to us if we hadn't left when we did. "

"I'm going to add what you just said to what I've already written," Phyllis said. She wrote hurriedly for a few moments before reading aloud a new portion of her journal:

We were preparing for bed in our vehicles in spite of the crowds around us. Alfred, undaunted by the crowds milling around, had set up his camp cot on top of the jeep and was readying his beg-bag, when suddenly a line of lanterns in the shape of a dragon emerged from a street at the other end of the town square where we were and came bobbing towards us. There was a stirring of excitement in the crowd. Fire-crackers were set off around us, and people bowed down and worshipped as the men carrying the glowing lanterns passed by with short, running steps.

Then unexpectedly the dragon stopped, and over the heads of the surging mass of people, we saw the lanterns return to us. They went back and forth, and the crowd was getting more and more excited. A tenseness was growing. What might happen? We were all wondering.

When Alfred quietly showed up at the jeep door with his cot and bed-bag, that's when I felt fear. "We're leaving immediately," he said.

Then with our headlights blazing on the crowd, the convoy pulled out, one vehicle after the other, and headed for open country. We drew up a mile or two away, near the ferry we had to cross the next morning. We stopped not far from a few shacks where the ferrymen lived. So quiet and still it seemed, bathed in the soft grey moonlight that brought a dim, misty glow from the river. Through the dark outlines of the trees on the bank, we could see across the fields to the city, and hear its raucous murmur far into the night. This time we had had to retreat from the battle against dark powers. This time we had not been able to proclaim the Good News. But

God had kept us safe to proclaim His Word another time in another place.

*   *   *

Six long weeks after it started, the Bible Convoy finally arrived in Sian, and Phyllis wrote her final journal entry:

We made Wukong last night, too tired for words to express. Our night all together on the *kang* bed in the inn passed by better than anticipated. At Sienyang we had lunch, and the men shaved and clipped, so we arrived in Sian rather decent looking. It truly was good to drive up the dusty wide street of the West Suburb, and in through the huge old gates. When we arrived at the mission late this afternoon, a great host of Christians was there to welcome us on this last day of March. What a triumphal feeling! Praise God!

*   *   *

Abbie's Journal
Oct 14, 2004
. . .today I made photo copies for my kids and Phil's of the little book of Dad's from my China boxes titled Bible Convoy, *authored by Phyllis Thompson, published by CIM in 1949. I remember reading it years ago when Dad first showed it to me. Since I'm researching for my own writing, I just read it again and am so fascinated that I just have to pass on copies to Dad's grandkids, along with some of his old photos from the convoy that I recently found in one of his neatly labeled envelopes (sure wish he had labeled ALL his photos).*

. . . *Phyllis's account so vividly describes their convoy experiences – how one of the trucks loaded with the precious cargo of Bibles capsized in a river; their struggles over miles and miles of nearly impassable muddy roads; how God protected them from bandit robbers and roaming rebel soldiers (often worse than bandits;, their frightening encounters with superstition and evil; dangerous river crossings over broken and bombed bridges and by scary ferries; enduring relentless rain; joyful meetings with Chinese Christians and sad meetings with people in desperate plights who knew nothing about the Good News of Jesus Christ; successful evangelistic street meetings; and so much more, including Sian's impending evacuation because of the civil war between the Nationalists and the Communists. . .*

Chapter 13

Abbie's Journal
Aug 8, 2004

. . . *several years ago for a library writing group, I wrote a memoir about Chengtu, the last stronghold for the Nationalists who were defeated in China's civil war against Communism. I'm reading at an open mic next week during a banquet for writers, and I decided to read my Chengtu piece. Earlier today I printed it from my files. As I did so, I thought about Grampa Nils who died so far away in Iowa while we were temporarily living in Chengtu. When Dad read the letter from his brother Oliver about their father's death and funeral, he shook with sobs. That was one of very few times I remember seeing Dad weep. Another time is in this memoir story. . .*

<u>My 1949 Chengtu Memoir</u>

"Go," my father Alfred said to Young Chu, our cook, who had insisted on accompanying us as we fled from the bombings and devastations of war.

"Go home, my brother. The time has come for you to leave us. Take your wife and your precious daughter and return to our home beside the Great Long River to live. I have heard the fighting is over there. Should anyone question you, here, here is the deed to Great House with the magistrate's chop. Hide it in your inner clothes. Please go, Young Chu – go now before they take you away because you are our friend."

Soon after I heard my father say those words, Cook and his wife and their little daughter left.

Now sixty years later, I see them again with memory's eyes. Cook was carrying all their belongings in two woven baskets that hung heavily from the ends of a stout bamboo pole balanced across his shoulders. Behind him, his wife carried a smaller bamboo pole loaded with food, their young daughter tied to her back. Her name was Heavenly Gift, but we always called her Mei-mei, Little Sister.

Looking down at us, Mei-mei laughed and waved to my brother Philly and me. Mei-mei had lived all her short life with us and didn't understand she was leaving. I wonder if she missed us as much as we missed her. I wonder if she grew up, married and had children who still live beside the Great Long River. I wonder if she is a believer.

"Never forget True God loves you. Always trust Him," my father said in farewell to the man who had been his loyal friend since their boyhood days together in Fengshan.

I felt pangs of fear and sadness when I saw tears running down my father's cheeks and onto his shirt. My mother tried to say something, but only choked sobs came out as she bowed to Cook's wife, our housemaid, who was like my mother's dear younger sister.

"Shieh shieh. Thank you, thank you, thank you," Cook and his wife murmured, bowing and politely backing away from us. "You have been too generous with us, much more than we deserve. We will never forget you, our foreign family. We will pray to True God of Heaven to bring us together again when the war is over."

I ran alongside them for a ways, calling out in Chinese to travel in peace and return safely to us soon. When Dad whistled to me from the gate where he was watching, I waved a last goodbye, then ran back to our compound, where we would soon be under compound arrest.

Cook was one of my special friends, and for a long

time I felt a huge sadness inside me for him and his family. Back then, I didn't know they were gone from our lives forever.

I remember how Cook boiled our sugar to remove bugs and dirt. When it was clean and cool, he gave me sweet brown lumps to suck. Often he took me with him to the street market to shop for the vegetables and meat he cooked for our rice meals. In the evenings after the outside lanterns were lit, I liked to sit with him and his family beside our cool stone water cistern. Sometimes my parents and others joined us.

Cook liked me too. For his wedding, I remember wearing a new red silk Mandarin jacket and pants embroidered with lotus flowers. I felt so proud to stand with my father beside my friend and his shy, pretty bride.

After they left Chengtu, my family never again heard from Cook and his family. But since China is so much more open these days, maybe someday our families' descendants will somehow reunite. . .

Chungtu, Szechwan, China, 1950
Year of Tiger

For eleven futile days, Alfred rode his bicycle early in the morning to the People's Republic Government Center in Chungtu. Daily he filled out tedious forms, some the same as previous days, and responded to hours of interrogation about his work and friends in China. Each morning as he cycled warily through the busy streets, alert for hostile Chinese, he prayed he would answer all questions truthfully and yet not incriminate himself, his family or other missionaries and Chinese Christians. He wished he could pretend not to be fluent in Chinese, but he was too well-known for that, and often called a "white Chinese." Prior to the Communists, that term was a compliment, but not these days.

On the twelfth morning, his persistence and careful evasiveness were rewarded. He was grudgingly granted an officially stamped exit permit to depart China with his family, traveling via Cheungking and Shanghai, and supposedly with government protection. As he bowed to express his thanks, he was sternly ordered to board a military plane flying to Cheungking that very afternoon, time uncertain.

Frantically, Alfred pedaled back to the mission compound where his family and other missionaries were living under "compound arrest," meaning they had to check in and out with the soldiers now positioned at the gate.

"Meggie, Meggie" he called out as he ran up the stairs to their room. "We're leaving right away! Praise Almighty God!"

The other missionaries in the house heard him and came from their rooms to hurry with him to Meggie. She was crying as she pulled suitcases from under their beds, suitcases they had kept packed and ready for fleeing at a moment's notice for years now. Wiping the tears from her cheeks with her hands every few seconds, she pulled clothes from a dresser drawer. Their friends helped Abbie and Philly dress quickly in several more layers of clothing, including sweaters and jackets. Alfred and Meggie did likewise. Their fleeing suitcases were small, and contained mainly medical items, canned foods, and bedding. Meggie's also contained framed photos of her four precious children, and a chamber pot.

"We're ready then," Alfred said. He and his family looked around their temporary home. They had already fled too many times to be leaving much. He knew Abbie and Philly would like to take the few toys and books they'd acquired here in Chengtu, especially Philly's first tricycle, but they knew fleeing meant not toys.

"Mommy and I will get you nice new toys and books when we get to Hong Kong," he said, putting his arms reassuringly around them. Sober-faced, they both nodded their heads.

"Please – pray – with – us – now," Meggie said, barely able to speak through her sobs.

The other missionaries gathered protectively around the Newquist family, and three of them prayed short prayers. Prayers for safe travel for the Newquists. Prayers that the rest of them would soon be granted exit permits. And prayers for their Christian friends who were already suffering persecution under China's new Communist government.

As the four Newquists hurried to the compound gate to get pedicabs to take them to the military airfield, they heard their missionary friends singing the farewell song: "God be with you til we meet again." And Alfred thought, *How many times have I been comforted by that song? Thank you, Almighty God!*

*   *   *

Cheungking

Two days after arriving in Cheungking, Alfred was permitted to purchase deck tickets for a boat powered by engines traveling down the Yangtze to

Shanghai. He was briskly told the boat was scheduled to depart the next day, but the time was unsure. So he and Meggie and the children would need to arrive at the dock early in the morning. He had hoped to get a cabin for the four of them, but cabin tickets were sold out, or so he was told. He suspected they were only sold out for "foreign devils with ugly noses and ghost eyes" like himself.

His heart was heavy as he bounced along in the pedicab speeding him back to the mission center. The center would soon close for good since the Chairman Mao's government was confiscating all missionary and church properties, or at least most of them. He and his family were some of the last missionaries leaving China, and while everything these days seemed dangerous, at least the bombings and gun battles had ceased. A year ago, Alfred had pondered staying indefinitely, but the choice was no longer his. The government had evicted all foreigners, and even imprisoned some.

Alfred sighed deeply and sadly. He looked around with compassion at the war-impoverished city. *Poor poor China*, he thought, *whatever will become of my motherland this time? And my three million Christian brothers and sisters, whatever will happen to you? Oh Almighty God, please grant them each one your special strength and grace in the dark days ahead. And also to my family as we head down the River tomorrow, according to Your will. . .*

*   *   *

The next morning as the sun was rising, Alfred and his family looked quietly at an awakening city while two pedicabs hurried them towards the next step on their journey to freedom. As usual, Alfred was on the lookout for anyone appearing hostile. Suddenly, a man swirling a gun jumped from the street curb and in front of the first pedicab, the one hauling Alfred and Abbie. As both pedicabs squealed to an abrupt stop, Alfred felt Abbie squeeze under his arm. She didn't say anything, but he could hear Meggie saying, "Oh God! Oh dear God!" And he knew she was sheltering little Philly with her body.

Praying urgently, Alfred pulled out the bag hanging around his neck inside his shirt. The bag contained their passports and other travel documents. But just as he reached inside for his government-issued travel protection papers, two armed soldiers appeared from nowhere. They quickly disarmed the man who kept yelling that foreign imperialists deserved to die, not escape. The soldiers gripped the man tightly between them, and one of the soldiers said to Alfred, "Our apologies, sir! Continue on your way. May you reach your homeland safely."

After the pedicabs moved on, Alfred thought, *Who were those soldiers anyway? Where did they come from? They saved our lives. Thank you, Almighty God!*

As they neared the dock and stopped, Meggie called to Alfred, "Oh dear God, look at all those people! How we will ever be able to get on the boat?"

Hundreds of Chinese people were jammed on the dock, pushing and shoving to clamber up barrels stacked alongside the boat like giant steps. *These people, too, were refugees*, thought Alfred, *fleeing from China's new government or saying farewell to someone who is. These were bad days for those who had had associations with foreigners, or even worse, with Chiang's Nationalists.*

He helped his family down from the pedicabs and quickly paid the pedicab drivers, not forgetting to give each of them a Gospel tract along with a word to trust in Jesus. Then he guided Meggie and the children to what seemed like a safe spot.

"Wait here," he said. "I'll board first and get a place for us on deck. You can board when the crowd clears and you can see the gang plank. I'll be watching you, and if you can't make it before the boat leaves, I'll come back to you. Try not to worry. Just keep praying."

He gave Meggie her passport and permits from his bag. She tucked them into her bra on top of the gold and silver coins already there.

"No one will dare reach in there to steal them from me," she said, and patted Alfred on his cheek. He nodded. Neither of them smiled.

*   *   *

Abbie watched her father push through the crowd with his suitcase and briefcase hanging from his shoulders with ropes he had tied to the handles. Soon she couldn't see him. But before long, she saw him again, climbing up the barrels, then over the railing and onto the deck. He turned and waved at them, whistled his piercing whistle, and pointed to the gang plank.

"Let's go, Mommy," she said. "Daddy whistled for us."

Just then, the boat's horn blew loud and long.

"Yes, we have to board right away," Meggie said. "But it's still such a mob. We'll have to hold tightly to each other so we don't get separated. That means I can't carry my suitcase. Open your suitcase, Abbie, hurry!"

Meggie opened her suitcase, pulled out the framed photos she carried everywhere, and pushed them into Abbie's suitcase. She also took out the potty and tied it around her waist with a scarf. She kicked her suitcase aside and grabbed her Abbie's and Philly's hands.

"Hold tight to your suitcases, but especially to me" she said to her children. "But if you drop them, just let them go so we don't fall."

Abbie felt herself dragged up the gangplank and onto the ship's deck. She was so frightened that she or Philly might become "lost" like their two older brothers. That they might end up living as orphan beggars along the river. While she was imagining that in her terror, the next thing she knew her father was gently releasing the handle of her suitcase from her hand and helping her sit down on the blanket he had spread on the deck.

"This is our home for the next few days," he said with a small smile. "We can pretend we're camping. We're so fortunate to be traveling on a boat with engine so it will only take us days instead of weeks to reach Shanghai. When I was boy and we traveled on this river, the boats had sails and often trackers had to pull us along, especially when we were going upriver."

*   *   *

By their second day traveling down the river, Abbie and her family were stunned to silence by the grotesquely swollen bodies swirling in the dark turbulent waters below their deck. They were tired, and sickened by the terrible sights and smells of the recent war still obvious on the riverbanks. When Abbie asked her mother why she always sat with her back to the river, Meggie answered that she couldn't bear to see the dead people in the water.

Abbie wanted to comfort her and said, "But they look like floating dolls, not real people." Her mother just nodded, and kept sitting with her back against the deck rails.

Mid-morning and mid-afternoon each day, cabin boys from the ship's gallery walked the decks selling hot, boiled water to drink, cooked rice, and sometimes tofu and vegetables. Alfred always bought some food and water, but Abbie noticed that some of the people around them never bought anything. Her child's heart felt sorry for the children, and so she whispered to her father to buy something for those children.

He whispered back, "I'm sorry for them, too, Abbie dear. But I just don't have enough money to get something for all of them. But if you keep watching carefully, you'll see they have brought food along to eat, but they only eat when it's dark so other can't see them eat and ask for food."

Abbie still felt sorry for them. She tried to talk with some of them, but nobody replied to her greetings. They wouldn't even look at her.

"Leave them alone, Abbie," her mother eventually told her. "They're afraid someone will see them talking with you. Remember we've told you how China's new government doesn't like Americans."

"But I'm from China," Abbie said. "I was born here like they were. Besides, I don't even remember America. So how do they know I'm from America?"

"By your appearance," her father answered.

"Don't you realize how different you look from everyone around us?" But I know how you feel. I used to feel the same way when I young like you."

Just then Philly cried out, "Look at that big big fish. It jumped out of the water."

"Why, sure enough, a river dolphin," his father said. The three of them stood at the railing and watched a small school of dolphins swim alongside the boat for awhile. Meggie didn't join them.

"There aren't many dolphins left these days," Alfred said to his children. "I suppose because of the war and pollution in the river. When I was boy, we used to see quite of few of them. Some Chinese catch them to eat. But most Chinese leave them alone because they think they're magical."

"How, Daddy? How are they magical?" Abbie asked, leaning over the railing, hoping to see the dolphins again, and ignoring the occasional bobbing body.

Meggie reached over and grabbed Abbie's skirt. "Don't lean over too far, young lady" she said. "We don't want to lose any more children."

Alfred answered Abbie's question. "Some Chinese believe that dolphins are people who died drowning and came back to life as dolphins. Being a dolphin is another life for them so they can try again for heaven. And because they've already died and come back to life as a dolphin, they have special powers that make them magical. So some Chinese think if you are kind to the dolphins, they'll help you. If you hurt them, then bad luck will happen to you. Something like their beliefs about the eight immortals."

Abbie said, "That sounds silly. But if it's true, there'll soon be lots more dolphins." And she pointed to the bodies in the river.

Abbie saw her mother frown at her father before saying to her, "Since we're Christians, dear, of course, we don't believe that. Now, how about a reading lesson? You haven't had one for several days."

Alfred sat down next to Meggie on their blanket and pulled his Gideon New Testament from his shirt pocket. Abbie snuggled up to him on one side, and Philly snuggled up to their mother on the other.

"Here's a story about Jesus and a lake," Alfred said, turning the pages in Matthew. "I'll read it first and then you can read it, Abbie. As you listen, Philly, keep in mind you'll soon be having reading lessons too. As soon as you're five."

"I can read it first," Abbie said. "I already know all the words in Matthew."

"Do you? That's fine. Then go ahead. Start here." Alfred pointed to chapter 14, verse 22. "After you read to the end of the chapter, I'll ask each of you a question, including Mommy. And Abbie, because you're reading, you can ask me a question."

When Abbie's reading was over and Alfred's questions had been answered and discussed, Abbie said, "Okay, I have a question for you, Daddy. It's kind of from this reading. Why didn't Jesus have any girl disciples?"

Alfred looked at Abbie with surprise on his face and said, "But Jesus did have girl and women disciples, many of them. You know the stories about them."

"Show me in your Bible, Daddy," Abbie said.

"First of all, let me explain two words for you, disciples and apostles. Then I'll show you some of the verses in the Gospels that mention Jesus' girl disciples."

*   *   *

Often during the rest of the boat trip and then the train trip from Shanghai to Hong Kong, Abbie asked to read or hear stories about Jesus' girl disciples. One afternoon on the train as she was looking out the window and thinking about the stories, she realized she was a disciple of Jesus, too. And that her parents weren't just missionaries, they were special traveling disciples, like the apostles.

But she wasn't sure about her brother, so she asked him, "Philly, are you a disciple of Jesus?"

Philly was playing with the one toy he carried in his fleeing suitcase, a little metal jeep. He was making motor noises when Abbie asked him. For several seconds, he kept on pushing his jeep along the seat and not answering. When he paused, he looked at her and said, "Sure, why wouldn't I be? We're a family of disciples." Then he went back to pushing his jeep up and down some imaginary hills.

Abbie saw her parents look at each other. They didn't say anything, but she knew from the looks on their faces that they were smiling inside.

The next day, the four of them climbed stiffly down from the train. Along with hundreds of Chinese who were also weary and grimy and ragged war survivors, they walked past the border guards and over Liberty Bridge into free Hong Kong.

Meggie was crying and repeating over and over, "Oh God, oh dear God, thank you, God."

One of the guards said, "Just listen to that crazy white woman."

Mean soldier, Abbie thought. She rudely looked him straight in the eyes and struck her forefinger several times against her cheek in the Chinese manner to shame him. The guard just laughed at her and spat on the ground.

Meggie quickly covered Abbie's mouth with her hand. "Shh, don't say anything," she warned. "We don't want to be detained here. Look, over there, look who's here to meet us."

The four of them staggered over to their waving, smiling relatives and friends, and to a new, free life.

*   *   *

Abbie's Journal
Sep 1, 2004

. . . for our anniversary dinner last evening, we went to Tao Chen's here Windridge. I had the vegetable soup (theirs is exquisite!) with extra pickled cucumber lettuce slices. I don't even have to ask for it anymore because they know me so well. As I was enjoying it, a long ago memory came back to me and I shared it with Dan – about going with my Chinese girlfriend on the compound in Chengtu into a basement-like place where there were huge earthen vats with vegetables soaking in pickling liquids. There was one I especially liked, still do, and my friend would reach into the pot with her fingers and give me one or two. I think she was a daughter of a servant there, but I'm not sure. I knew I was doing something wrong, because I wasn't supposed to eat anything that my parents didn't know about. But oh, those pickles were so good, and I was too young to realize I could easily die from dysentery, just like my two "lost" brothers. After all these years, I still feel sad I didn't have time to tell her "goodbye" that day we left Chengtu so quickly. . .

Chapter 14

Abbie's Journal
May 10, 2005
. . . a few weeks ago, my <u>real</u> cousins, Aunt Abigail and Uncle Nathan's kids, started an online, round-robin sharing about our time on Cheung Chau Island. We were refugees there after our families escaped from Communist China. And my goodness, what fun memories we've been resurrecting about a place and time we all remember as idyllic, probably because of how horrific our lives had been until then. . .
. . . just off the Hong Kong coast, in 1950 that tiny island was hilly, and scattered with bombed ruins of large summer houses. On one side was a low, flat area with a Chinese village, whose population made a bleak living by fishing, once supplemented by serving the former vacationers. The ruins and hills and caves were a wonderful playground for Phil and me and our cousins. How we enjoyed the freedom to roam safely for the first time in our lives. One or two hours a day, our parents took turns guiding us through some schoolwork and Bible stories. But mostly, we played and explored, free from fear of soldiers and bandits and gunfire and bombs and dead people. . .

Hong Kong, British Territory, 1950
Year of Tiger

Meggie couldn't stop staring at the new missionary with the lovely curly blond hair seated in the front of the room. She wished the missionary leading the evening devotions would hurry and close so she could meet the newcomer.

Deloris was the newcomer's name, and Meggie was drawn to her bright attractiveness. Looking at her, Meggie felt a stab of homesickness for America and the friendship of women like this one who obviously hadn't lived through years of deadly, devastating wars. Everything about her was new and healthy looking. Meggie still felt like weeping from the glorious music that had flowed from Deloris's golden trumpet before the message. Why oh why, she wondered, was the mission board allowing young, single women like this one to come to China during this dreadful time of war. Didn't they realize what might happen to them?

Meggie pushed away the thought that often tempted her, that sometimes sacrifices for God were just too much. She gently shifted little Philly who was asleep on her lap, and stretched her legs.

Abbie, leaning against her father Alfred, was reading a book. She looked up with a frown when Philly's foot bumped her book. But smiled at her mother when she saw her brother was sleeping and not teasing.

When Brother Julius announced the final prayer, Meggie was proud that Abbie, though only eight, closed her book without prompting and bowed her head. As soon as the chorus of "Amen's" ceased, Meggie stood and handed her sleeping son to his father.

"I just want to chat a bit with the new missionary," she said. "I won't be long."

She walked quickly away from her family, but not before she saw the smile that passed between father and daughter as they sat back down. Abbie again leaned against her father and opened her book.

* * *

The next morning at breakfast, Abbie saw the new missionary lady look around and then head towards their table.

"Mommy," she whispered. "I think the new missionary is coming to our table to eat with us."

"Good," her mother said. "I invited her last night to join us."

Smiling happily, Meggie introduced her family. "This is Auntie Deloris," she said to Abbie and Philly. "When we go to Formosa after Christmas, she's going too. So this is a good time to get to know each other."

Deloris sat in the chair next to Abbie. "What a pretty name you have," she said leaning down to Abbie's level.

Abbie grinned. "It's the same as my daddy's sister."

"Is it? How special," Deloris said, and winked at her. "I haven't met your Aunt Abigail yet. But I will tomorrow. Your mother invited me to go with your family to Cheung Chau Island for a visit."

Abbie grinned again and nodded. She couldn't remember anyone winking at her before, but she had read about it in stories. Next time she was in front of a mirror, she was going to see if she could do it. She had a happy feeling for this new mission auntie. So to keep her attention, she asked, "Is your name the same as one of your real auntie's?"

"No," Aunt Deloris said. "It's just a name that my mother and father liked. And my older brothers liked it too."

"My older brothers got lost in China," Abbie said. "But not Philly and me."

"Oh no!" Deloris said. "That's so very sad. Nobody told me." She looked up at Meggie and Alfred, who were looking at Abbie with concern on their faces.

"Abbie dear," her mother said, "lost is a way of saying died. Your older brothers died from sickness during all the fighting. Their bodies are buried in China, but their souls are with Jesus. I thought you knew that."

Abbie shook her head. "I don't remember you saying they died, Mommy. I just remember about Donny and Kilby being lost."

She leaned her head back against the chair and closed her eyes. But a few seconds later, she looked at her parents and said happily, "That means they're in heaven. That's much better than being with all those starving orphan Chinese children, lost from their parents because of the bombings. I'm glad you explained."

"We would have explained sooner if we'd known you didn't understand," Alfred said.

"You always look sad when you look at their pictures," Abbie said, "so I just don't talk about them."

When they were nearly finished breakfast and Abbie and Philly were listening to Aunt Deloris tell them about her family America, Abbie heard her father say to her mother in a low voice, "We must be sure she understands about the boys."

Abbie couldn't hear what her mother said, but she saw her parents' eyes and mouths. When they looked like that, it made her tummy feel strange even though right now their new Auntie Deloris was making her and Philly laugh.

*   *   *

The next day, Abbie sat close to the side of the motorboat taxi, trailing the fingers of one hand in the warm, dark blue ocean water. With her other hand, she held tightly to a canopy poll. She loved water – the ocean and rivers and lakes and swimming pools. Her father said she was just like her grandmother. Abbie was glad, and hoped she wouldn't grow up to be like her own mother, who often threw-up when they were in a boat and was afraid to swim in deep water.

She looked at her mother who was lying on a bench with her head on a blow-up army pillow and a blanket pulled up over her face. *Poor Mommy*, she thought.

Even the awful boat trip down the Yangtze River war hadn't changed Abbie's feelings about water. Even though she tried not to remember it, she still had bad dreams about all those dead bodies floating in the river, and about the piles of mangled bodies in the streets from the war. Her parents told her they thought the bad dreams would go away when they reached safe Formosa, and to trust God Who was always with her, especially when she was afraid.

Philly's arms weren't long enough for him to touch the water. So he sat looking quietly between Aunt Deloris and her father who were talking to each other. That's something Abbie liked as much as playing with water – listening to grownups talk.

Aunt Deloris was asking, "So Alfred, why are your sister and her family staying on Cheung Chau instead of in Hong Kong at the missionary center with the rest of us?"

He answered, "Oh, you'll see. It's a beautiful place to live these days compared to Hong Kong, especially for a family."

Deloris started to say something, but he continued, "Lots of great areas for the children to run and play, even some clean, grassy areas. And a nice swimming beach as well. Meggie and I want to join Abigail and Nathan while we prepare for Formosa. Did you know Cheung Chau used to be a vacation spot for the wealthy? During the war with Japan and the occupation, many of the houses were bombed. Fortunately, a few nice ones are left. The British government is allowing Western refugees from China like us to stay in them while we're in transition."

Oh goodie, Abbie thought. *I'd rather be on an island in the ocean than in that tall building crowded with people and no yard. And our cousins will be there to play with. We haven't seen them since China. Maybe we'll do lessons together. That's more fun than lessons by myself.*

Just then her father said, "Abbie, take your hand out of the water now to be safe. We're getting close to Cheung Chau. We'll be docking soon."

Abbie obeyed at once, smiling in his direction. She liked pleasing her parents.

*   *   *

Abbie's Journal
May 15, 2005
. . . yesterday I reminded my cousins and Phil in our round-

robin email how the highlight of each day on Cheung Chau came when young Chinese herders guided their grazing cows past our play palaces and forts. As we saw the cows nearing, excitedly we would warn each other in English and Chinese – the cows are coming! the cows are coming. Then frightened by the monstrous horns and hooves of the cows, we scrambled frantically up to the top of large boulders before bravely brandishing our stick weapons at the cows. And we although we tried to obey our parents and ignore the herders' taunts of small foreign devils, small foreign devils, we sometimes naughtily teased back, first checking to make sure no adults were listening – monkey face, monkey face. Our hearts obviously didn't yet have our parents' missionary zeal. . .

. . . eventually we relocated to Taiwan, known back then to Westerners as Formosa. Aunt Deloris and several other single missionaries were part of our group, the first in our mission to follow the Nationalist government of Chiang Kai-shek there, and we were formally welcomed by President Chiang. Aunt Abigail and her family didn't come for another year or two. . .

. . .in the 1950s, after fifty years of Japanese occupation, Taiwan's cities and towns were still developing. Its paved roads were few, dirt and gravel roads many. Faucets and running water were rare, water from wells and cisterns common. Indoor sit-down flush toilets were unknown, outdoor and indoor squat toilets the norm. Yep, that's how I still remember Hwalien. After taking a ship from Hong Kong to Keelung, we flew from Taipei to Hwalien in an old army airplane with its door missing. Imagine that happening today! We sat in bucket seats against the sides of the plane, with our belongings piled on the floor in front of us. Poor Mom kept her eyes shut most of the time and missed the fun of looking down from the open doorway at the movie-like

scenes of our new country's mountains and beaches and scary-looking Suao Highway. . .

President Chiang Kai-shek welcomes "Alfred"
(front right) and other missionaries to Formosa in 1951.

PART THREE

1951 to 1959

Chapter 15

**A letter home from Meggie
Hwalien, Formosa
1951, Year of Hare**

October 24, 25, 1951
My own dearest Mother and Dad,

My head is so heavy – I feel so weary – oh how I LONG to just sit down and chat with you! But I want you to know we are safe and still have our little home – all because you constantly PRAY!

I wrote those above words yesterday. Today I WILL finish this letter to you, so Alfred can take it to the American Military officer he meets with regularly to mail letters to you by APO (how we thank God for this privilege).

We have just had one of the most terrifying experiences we have ever undergone. But even though our bodies are still trembling, we have peace of heart. I remember years ago little Donny whispering to me as bombs fell around us in Sian, "Mommy, my heart is shivering in my lungs." And that is the way I have felt for days now while praying for God to have mercy on all of us, especially on our dear Abbie and Philly.

It all began about 5:30 in the morning three days ago when we were awakened by quite an earthquake shock. We have been told to expect about 364 shocks a year on this island, and we had had none until then. But that morning it seemed the earth was making up for lost time as we had shock after shock.

Mid-morning, our dear missionary friend Deloris came rushing on her bicycle to warn us that around noon we would have more and worse shocks, and to make preparations. How does one go about preparing for earthquakes!

When the tremors started again, we all headed for the front door. Suddenly, the walls seemed to meet us on all sides and hurtle hunks of plaster at us. The door kept changing its position, but finally, we were all outside in an open area, safe and unhurt, but gasping and sobbing. From then on, there was nothing more we could do while the earth shook violently and cracked open, except to PRAY!

Mercifully, we were spared not only from the tragedies that did happen, but also from seeing and hearing much. Down in the main city of Hwalien, people were buried alive and many were wounded. But up here on our hillside, we were comparatively safe. In the afternoon when the shocks subsided, our Formosan housegirl, Bee-lee, rushed home to see her family in Hwalien. Later she told us how she saw dreadfully mangled bodies being unearthed. We were thankful for our simple little Japanese house which was constructed to withstand earthquakes. But even so, we didn't dare go back inside, nor did hundreds of our neighbors around us who were moaning and wailing to the gods.

As if the earthquake had not made enough misery, it began to rain. We prayed God to stop it, since so many were without homes or afraid to go inside. There were warnings of more shocks to come, so Alfred fixed us a little bamboo and wooden shelter, and we were able to get some rest. The rain did stop, and I sat by their sides while the children slept, praying over and over, "Please God, protect these two we have left. Please God, do not take any more of our children. Oh dear God, dear God, give me enough strength and courage for what is ahead."

I could hear not far away the constant, menacing rumble of the sea and then felt one shock after another. I could not sleep, and not long after midnight our little street seemed to be suddenly very full of traffic. By dawn, more and more people were coming, carrying their bundles, and hurrying, hurrying to escape a new menace – a crumbling of the sea coast or a tidal wave was expected!

Feeling I could scarcely bear any more, we quickly wakened Abbie and Philly. Taking blankets, raincoats, and some food, Be-lee and the children and I hurried after the fleeing people, leaving Alfred to come later with our passports and other valuables on his bicycle. A few miles from our house, we met some of our missionary and American military friends on a knoll of a high hill, including Deloris whom the children dearly love because of her extraordinary personality. We felt safe there and settled to wait. It was like waiting for Jesus to come – the song "Sunrise Tomorrow" kept coming to me!

For hours and hours, people kept coming, bearing their heavy burdens of possessions, and carrying children and the elderly on their backs. Rumors of what was to happen continued to spread, including the stories of whose who for one reason or another could not escape from their homes and expected to be swallowed up by the sea or the angry openings in the earth. We waited and prayed, though we scarcely knew what words to pray. Deloris cheered us all with a concert of hymns on her trumpet, and we shared the Good News of the Gospel with the hundreds around us, people whose ears were now receptive.

At long last, Alfred came to tell us the danger was past. Suddenly, the knoll seemed very, very beautiful. We ate the food we had brought, enjoying an unexpected and wonderful picnic. On the way home, we wondered how our home had fared. Amazingly, nothing was gone, though every door stood wide open. In the whole devastated area, there was no looting - just one of many ways that Formosa is different from China, for the people are not survival-desperate.

We did give away some precious blankets. But the families we gave them to needed them for their children more than we did, and so we refused to accept them back. Before we got home, another drenching rain came, soaking everyone and everything. But the danger was over - there were after-quakes from time to time, but the earth was settling down again for the time being.

How wonderful to be back in our home, even though plaster has fallen, and the electricity and water are not yet on! Today the sun is shining. We have our bedding and clothes out on bamboo poles and bushes. By the time you receive this letter, our little house will be shipshape again. We are surprised how normal and peaceful things already are.

But there are other earthquakes shaking this

world of ours. Behind the Iron Curtain in China, the earth is quaking and shaking in rebellion against the Truth of our calling. Once again our lives have been spared for God's purposes, though as we know too well, in death God's purposes are also fulfilled.

Frightening experiences always make me LONG to be with you! How we love you, and pray each day that you our loved ones so far away may also be kept safe – safe especially from the quakes of the evil one.

Please type copies with carbons of this letter as usual, and send them to our list.

Lovingly,
Your Meggie, Alfred, and our dear Abbie and Philly

II Tim. 1:7 – For God has not given us a spirit of fear, but of power and of love and of a sound mind.

Many were killed and injured in the
1951 disastrous Hwalien earthquake.

"Alfred," "Abbie" and "Philly" haul water in Hwalien
after the 1951 earthquake damaged the running water pipes.

Chapter 16

Abbie's Journal
July 27, 2006
. . . Yikes –a frightening flashback to my Hwalien childhood this morning long before daylight! A sudden shaking awakened me, and for a second I lay stunned. Then with a long-ago trained reflex, I leaped out of bed and started to awaken Dan and rush us outside, but paused as the earthquake had already stopped. After a few moments, I snuggled back under the covers, wondering if I might have been dreaming.
. . . as soon as I got up several hours later, I checked the news, partly to prove myself correct to Dan who laughed off my account as impossible, until he heard the reports of the earthquake's scope and damage. Imagine! An earthquake here in the Midwest! And we are supposedly living over a fault, a somewhat newly discovered one – is that possible?
. . . at least I don't have to worry about our town falling into the ocean like I did when I was a child, when I was new to Taiwan and its frightening earthquakes that sometimes in fury swallowed buildings and people or caused tidal waves that did. But hey, guess our town could fall into Lake Michigan, the final "resting place" of thousands of sunken ships, people, and long forgotten treasures. . .
. . . we lived in the Hwalien area for two years. Then we moved to Taipei, where Phil and I enrolled in a real school for the first time. Talk about an adjustment to our "normal" home-schooling-anytime-convenient routine! Soon after we started in that school, I had my mouth taped shut for talking

too much. When my 7th grade teacher heard me joking about it later during recess, she clarified it wasn't a joke by making me write 100 times on the chalk board something about not talking when I shouldn't. And we wonder why some kids learn at school to dislike writing! Obviously, the punishment didn't harm my love of talking or writing! But I did learn never to be punished in school again. . .

Taichung, Formosa, 1957
Year of Monkey

The American military MAAG after-school bus stopped in front of their home on San Min Lu Road. Abbie and Phil waved goodbye as they stepped off. Several seconds after Abbie rang their gatebell, they heard their housekeeper Ah-man's voice calling, *"Lai-la, lai-la!* Coming!"

Ah-man opened the gate's bolt, then slid it shut behind them.

"A guest is here waiting for you, Young Miss," she said to Abbie. "I have already served her fresh doughnuts and tea."

Abbie smiled at Ah-man. "Thank you. Who is the guest?"

"The tall music lady with beautiful curly hair."

"Oh good!" Abbie said happily.

She and Philly hurried into the front room. "Hello, Aunt Deloris!" they said almost as one voice.

Abbie was smiling as she looked around the room. "Where's Mom? Did Ah-man tell her you're here?"

"Hi kids! Your Mom's at the radio studio sitting in for me," Deloris answered. "She sent me here to enjoy your afternoon snack with you. Plus, I have a favor to ask of you, Abbie. Say, how often does Ah-man make you these scrumptious doughnuts?"

"Every week," Philly said, smiling, his lips covered with sugar.

"Ah-man usually just cooks Chinese food and serves us fruit for our snacks," Abbie said after swallowing her first bite of a soft warm doughnut. "But her doughnuts are her one really delicious Western thing. And they're always perfect, like these. Aunt Abigail taught her to make them. When I ask Ah-man to teach me, she just laughs."

"So how are you two favorites of mine liking Morrison's new campus?" Deloris asked.

"It's so nice," Abbie said. "All of us love the big rooms and the huge grounds. The dorms are really special, not at all crowded like the old Japanese mansion. Of course, Philly and I won't be staying in the dorms as much as many of the kids do. But we'll like it when we do stay. We've already visited our friends' dorms. And the dining hall is almost like the NCO Club. Everyone says the cooks are better than last year's. Philly and I will eat lots of our meals there because Mom is teaching this year, as you know."

"I'm going to be teaching, too. Did your mom tell you yet?" Deloris asked.

Philly kept chewing, but he looked at Deloris when Abbie asked, "Teaching what?"

"Band!"

Abbie clapped her hands. "That's perfect! Now I know I'll take band. I wasn't sure I would because I heard someone else might be the director. None of us kids like him very much. Maybe you can teach Philly the trumpet like you did me when we lived together in Hwalien. He's old enough now."

Deloris turned to Philly. "Would you like that?"

"Sure," Philly said. "Abbie's already taught me how to blow and the scale. But I'll have to get another horn besides hers, and learn how to read notes."

"I'll find you a horn right away," Deloris said. "She patted both of them on their hands.

"Abbie," she continued, "the real reason I'm here is to ask you if I can borrow one of your dresses. You brought back such pretty ones from America last year. I have an important dinner to go to on short notice, so I don't have time for a new dress by a tailor. How about it?"

"Of course," Abbie said. "What's the dinner?"

"I guess it's okay to tell you. Your mom knows, and she suggested I borrow one of your dresses. I have a date with a China Airline pilot."

Abbie's eyes widened. "A Chinese?"

Deloris nodded.

"But that's not allowed, is it? Mom and Dad wouldn't let me date Bobby Lu last summer. They explained the mission rules to me."

Deloris nodded again and said, "I know. So I'm just going for this one last dinner with him. I really really like him. He's so nice and so handsome. We've become very good friends, too good, I guess. So I've decided to explain to him why I can't see him anymore. Of course, I could, but then I'd have to quit the mission. And I don't think that's God's will at this time."

As Abbie and Deloris walked to Abbie's

bedroom, Abbie saw the sad look in Deloris's eyes. She was glad to loan her dear friend her best dress. It was a sleeveless dress, a pale orange patterned chiffon over taffeta with a lovely swishy skirt. She hoped the dress would help Deloris have a special evening.

Aunt Deloris is going to be like Gladys Aylward, Abbie thought. *What a crazy mission rule. It doesn't even seem Christian, even if Mom and Dad say it is the right way because it turns out best, whatever that means.*

That night when Abbie was bed nearly asleep, she heard her parents talking softly in their bedroom about Deloris, and about the men she had refused to marry. Three were missionaries that Abbie knew who had married other women. *That's interesting,* she thought sleepily.

The last words she heard were her mother's. "Wouldn't you know it! The one man Deloris shouldn't marry is the only one she falls for. I'm afraid she'll end up single. But it won't matter. She's so talented and capable."

* * *

On Monday afternoon of Morrison's second week at the new campus, students and teachers looked out the front-facing classroom windows more often than usual. They'd been told the last hour today would be a special chapel. But that's all they knew so far.

About one-thirty, Abbie and the others saw a few visitors start to gather inside the front gate. The front wall with its gate was quite distance from the main classroom building, so it was difficult to see just who the visitors were, causing whispers and note passing among the students. The visitors appeared to be both missionaries and Chinese, something of a mystery for this time of day.

The day was extremely hot and humid, a typical early September day. Working on her chemistry in study hall, Abbie was sweating enough for her blouse to stick to the back of her chair in spite of the new electric fan in the room blowing at full speed. She knew she wasn't the only one who would leave school that day with brown varnish marks on her clothes. Looking out the window again, she hoped their chapel wasn't going to be held down by the gate. Dust was swirling in the air there as cars and pedicabs kept stopping to let out their passengers before parking.

"Okay, it's time get ready to leave for chapel in five minutes," Miss Cloer, the eleventh and twelfth grade study hall teacher, announced. "You probably saw the note delivered to me earlier. When the bell rings, you'll please follow me orderly, two by two, boys with boys and girls with girls, down to the front gate. Just the high school will attend this chapel. The younger students will remain in their classrooms with their teachers."

There were some groans. Abbie obviously wasn't the only one feeling the heat and dreading the dust. *Girls with girls! Boys with boys! Shucks!* She looked back at her boyfriend and squinted. He grinned back. No secret hand touching on the walk to the gate this time, their eyes said to each other.

Barb in the desk beside Abbie raised her hand.

"Yes?" Miss Cloer asked her.

"How do we stand when we get down there?" Barb asked.

"I'm not sure yet," Miss Cloer said. "But perhaps in a circle around the gate. My announcement note says this chapel is a prayer service."

"What? A prayer service down there?" Abbie blurted.

"Did you raise your hand, Abbie?" Miss Cloer asked.

"Oops! Sorry, Miss Cloer. I was so surprised."

Abbie waited a few seconds, then leaned over to Barb and whispered, "I bet it's something about the shrine beside the gate. My dad says it's a dangerous presence for us kids. You know, idols and demons and all that."

Barb nodded and whispered, "Walk with me?"

"Of course," Abbie whispered back.

Somehow the two girls' boyfriends managed to walk in line behind them. Abbie saw Miss Cloer raise her eyebrows at them, but she didn't say anything and even smiled a tiny smile. Probably because she hadn't gotten into any boy trouble yet, not like some of her friends. Abbie grinned. She didn't even want to get into trouble like that. She didn't just care about her parents finding out. She cared about God.

Someone by the front gate started a song as Morrison's principal, Chinese staff, high school teachers and students walked towards them. Soon more than fifty voices were singing together in English and Mandarin, "*Onward Christian soldiers, marching as to war, with the cross of Jesus, going on before. . .* "

By the time the first stanza had been sung, and the second and third stanzas mostly hummed with just a few singing the words loudly, a circle several people deep had formed around the shrine. The students were so used to seeing shrines that they hadn't paid much attention to this one as they passed back and forth through the new school's gate beside it. A few of them had probably wondered when it would be removed so the front wall could be finished. At least that's what Abbie and her boyfriend had wondered to each other one recent evening when they were standing in its shadow, secretly holding hands.

Now both of them and the others around them listened attentively as the chairman of the school board explained why they were meeting for this special service of Bible reading and prayer. They were here, he said, to ask God to bind the forces of evil the idol enclosed in the shrine represented, so that everyone coming and going past the shrine would be protected by God's Almighty hand until the shrine was removed. This Christians are instructed to do in the Bible passage, he said, which would now be read aloud in English and Mandarin. Following Scripture, two missionaries and two Chinese Christians prayed. Then all were dismissed.

Abbie was surprised at the huge crowd of onlookers that gathered around them while her eyes were closed and her head bowed. She and her boyfriend had to push their way through the onlookers as they headed back to the school building together for a French Club meeting. After French Club, Abbie had cheerleading practice, and her boyfriend, basketball practice.

Leaving the gate area, Abbie noticed some of the missionaries passing out Gospel tracts to the onlookers.

Dad would be doing that if he were here, she thought.

When she and her boyfriend passed the classroom windows where her mom was dismissing her second grade class, Abbie waved. Her mom waved back and tapped on the window. If Abbie had extra time after cheerleading practice before the supper gong chimed, she would come back and help her mom grade papers. Play practice was right after supper. Then she and her boyfriend would be together again back stage. Abbie couldn't help smiling at everyone they met as they hurried to Miss Cloer's classroom.

* * *

Supper that evening was more sober than normal. Idols and the dark spirit world were never joked about by missionary kids. Their families knew from experience how frightening the powers of darkness could be. Abbie and her friends agreed that whether they slept in the dorm or their own homes, this was a night to sleep with open Bibles on their pillows.

* * *

Abbie's Journal
Aug 6, 2007
. . . Deloris, my family's dear friend and mine, is 80 today! Hard to believe, as she's one of those "forever young" people! I'm thinking how fortunate I am to have had her as a special friend for so long. While God has allowed my life to be blessed by many wonderful women, she is right up there at the top with my Mom. When I was young in Taiwan, "Auntie" Deloris was one who helped guide my interest to the important, achieving women in the Bible, like judge Deborah, prophetess Ann, clever Abigail, and others. . .
. . . even though she was twenty years older, back then I considered her my best friend. Over the years, I had so much

fun swimming and picnicking and chatting with her in fun places like Sun Moon Lake, Taroko Gorge, the park in Taichung, etc. . .

. . . she taught both Phil and me to play the trumpet. And although I was far from the marvelous and famous musician she is, I sure enjoyed playing in bands and trios. She even "hired" me to work as her assistant for a couple of summers. I didn't find out until recently from Phil that the folks asked her to do that and paid my earnings. Oh well, it was still super fun to travel around with her help out with this and that. . .

. . . for years Aunt Deloris belonged to the same mission as my family, but then she branched out on her own and became the founder and director of ORTV. Because of her joyful, talented response to God's leadership call, through ORTV, she has influenced probably millions to learn about Christ, plus learn excellent English in the process. She went to China as a missionary at age 21 in 1948 (just imagine being that young and dropping into the midst of a devastating war from peaceful America). Today she lives permanently in Taiwan, but often travels to China and throughout the world. What a woman! Just ask anyone in Asia. . .

. . . a few years ago, Aunt Deloris asked me to write her biography in English. It's been written in Chinese. What a story hers is, for sure! After several years of thinking and praying about it, and feeling so inadequate to tell her powerful life story, I finally agreed. But by then, she had decided against it for various reasons. Her occasional phone calls and notes always inspire me. Yes! What a woman! Ten thousand fragrant birthday blessings, dear Aunt Deloris. . .

Chapter 17

Abbie's Journal
Sep 16, 2007

. . . *when I was growing up, I never wondered where Dad got the American Hershey chocolate candy bars he carefully divided up as special treats for our family. We rarely got more than one or two squares each, and then had the fun of seeing who could make theirs last the longest. Mom usually lost first, and Dad always won. . .*

. . . *now that I've been reading more of his journals and papers from my China boxes, I realize he probably got the candy bars from U.S. military officers when he had "chats" with them, sharing info he'd heard from his Chinese friends that he thought might be useful, and answering questions the U.S. officers had, especially when we lived in Hwalien. YUM, the deliciousness of those one or two small pieces of chocolates will always be a special memory, probably for Phil too. . .*

. . . *after we moved to Taichung, Mom got PX privileges because she taught at Morrison where U.S. military kids attended along with us MKs. Then we ate chocolate more often, and not just one or two small squares at a time. Even so, chocolate never lost being special, and hasn't to this day. However, I still can't eat a whole candy bar at once – something lifelong, I guess, like Dad's training us to chew every bite of food at least 20 times. . .*

Taichung Formosa, 1959
Year of Boar

"We absolutely cannot let Abbie do it," Alfred stated to Meggie for the third time that day.

"Of course not, I know that," Meggie answered. "And we both know once she gets to the States, it won't take her long to adjust and be happy. But oh, dear God, how can I bear for her to leave? Then, neither do I want her to stay and attend university here."

Alfred walked to the window and looked towards the gate. "I thought I heard the gate open," he said, "but I guess not."

Soon he continued, "We have to tell her today it's something we're just not going to discuss any further. It's wonderful she's been accepted at Chesterton College in Windridge where many of us Newquists have attended so happily. She needs to start thinking of it as a door opened by God. The hard thing is, I know exactly how she feels. I know how difficult it is to leave a country that seems like home and go so far away by yourself to another country that's supposed to be home, but doesn't seem like it."

After several minutes of quiet, Meggie said softly, "When she comes, you tell her. Oh Alfred, she's been such a good child, so easy all along. I'm sorry we have to go against her will on this. You can tell her the mission board probably wouldn't approve anyway. They'd probably say she might fall in love with, well you know. . . And we did have a scare last summer at Sun Moon Lake with that Bobby Lu guy. Remember him? I've always been glad Deloris was there to guide

Abbie so we didn't have to."

Alfred's eyes squinted in thought. Yes, he remembered. It was one of the greatest ironies of missionary life, as far as he was concerned – the rule about no romantic attachments or marriage with nationals. That would have to change. But he didn't want Abbie to be another test case. Deloris's experience had been unexpectedly painful and, yes, harmful.

"Maybe going on the island expedition with Ed and me this summer would help soothe her disappointment," he suggested. "What do you think?"

Meggie sighed, then nodded. "Yes, she'd love the adventure. You know how she is. And why not take Philly along as well? It may be their last summer together. If Philly goes, probably Ed would take Leif. The three kids can have fun together, and look out for each other when you and Ed are busy."

"They only thing is, they'll fill up the back of the jeep," Alfred answered. "I wasn't going to pull the trailer, but sure, I can pull it if they're along. At least we don't have to worry about bandits and soldiers like we did on the mainland."

"No, just headhunters," Meggie said.

When Alfred started to protest, she added, "I know, I know! Headhunting has been outlawed for years. I just hope they've heard that in the mountain areas you'll be exploring. You'll be the first white people many of those tribal people have ever seen. They'll either want to worship you or kill you. Isn't that what Ed likes to say?"

*   *   *

Two weeks before, Abbie had graduated

valedictorian of her Morrison class. Not that it meant much, she realized, considering that fewer than half of them were left to graduate. The others had all gone to accredited high schools in the States for their last year of high school. But anyway, it had been fun wearing a lovely white brocade dress, and being surrounded by all those smiles and congratulations and presents. Plus being invited by friends to restaurants for several Chinese feasts with her favorite dishes – like Peking duck, garlic beans with deep-fried tofu, a whole fish in curry sauce, pickled vegetable soup, and of course, ending with eight precious foods sticky sweet rice.

Now she was the only one of her class still in Formosa. The others had already flown to the States, looking forward to summer jobs and living the real American life. They couldn't believe Abbie's reluctance to leave the island, nor had they been able to change her determination to stay as long as possible. So here she was alone with her family, and not all that happy about the future they were forcing on her. In her heart, she wondered if she was different from the others because she'd been born on the mainland.

Abbie figured the jeep trip around the island was her parents' way of saying they were sorry about not giving in to her pleadings. She'd discussed it with Aunt Deloris, who mostly just listened. By the time she finished her side, Abbie knew from Aunt Deloris's comments that she agreed with her parents. So Abbie resigned herself to the inevitable. At least she had her summer job as Aunt Deloris's assistant, plus now the round-island adventure to enjoy before she had to face her future.

*   *   *

Late into the night, Alfred made notes from his correspondence with Ed. The next day the two of them would be explaining to the field committee the details of their round-island trip. While the primary purpose of their expedition was to search for tribal communities without churches, he and Ed also planned to explore a mystery they had been intensely curious about ever since they first heard the tribal legend several years ago.

Both men were born and raised in China, the sons of missionaries called pioneers by many. He and Edvard Torjesen might have disagreed, insisting the true China pioneers were missionaries like Robert Morrison, James Hudson Taylor, or even their own fathers. However, Alfred acknowledged their lives often did have pioneer challenges, sometimes exciting ones, like this opportunity to research an ancient tribal legend and share the Gospel with people who had never heard about Jesus. Maybe their search would even bring him closer to the truth about the mysterious Stone Ten Keepers, even though this was no longer in China mainland.

He had told Abbie and Philly about the tribal legend last night after family devotions.

"What?" Abbie asked, her eyes wide and bright for the first time in days. "You mean Noah's Ark might be on the top of a mountain here in Formosa? But Dad, that doesn't fit with the Bible, does it?"

"You're right," he'd answered. "But Ed and I talked with tribesmen who were sure their ancient ancestors arrived here after a great flood that covered the world. They insisted their ancestors' boat still rests high on a mountain they call sacred. Interestingly, I've read that many cultures around the world have a legend like this one that echo the biblical account. I just never expected to find one here. It's one more mystery to solve if we can." He took off his glasses and rubbed his eyes, then shrugged his shoulders at Meggie who was frowning a bit.

"Can we kids climb on it if you find it?" Philly asked.

"Not if it's considered sacred by the tribes living around it," Alfred answered. "We'll have to decide that when we find whatever it is, if indeed we find anything."

*   *   *

A month later, the five of them set out on what Aunt Deloris had enviously told Abbie was a trip of a lifetime – a trip that would take them from the northern end of Formosa to the southern end, mostly along primitive coastal and mountain roads. Into Alfred's old US Army jeep that could traverse just about any terrain, they packed camping gear, carefully calculated supplies of water and food, a few clothes, and boxes of Gospels and salvation tracts.

Early in the morning, they started out from Hwalien on roads that for awhile were coarse pavement mixed with gravel. Those "good" roads didn't last long. Soon they were in the northeastern mountains. Here the roads were single-lane and rutted dirt, often right on the edge of steep precipices that plummeted to the ocean.

No wonder our mothers promised to pray for us

hourly when they said goodbye, thought Abbie, looking down at the wild white-peaked ocean waves far below. *Mom would be nervous to death if she were with us.*

But even adventure-loving Abbie welcomed nightfall by the end of each long day of hot, cramped and dusty riding in the jeep. Some nights they camped out, preparing simple meals from their supplies. Other nights, they enjoyed the luxury of baths and sleeping between sheets in missionary homes. But most nights, they stayed with tribal villagers, sleeping in their sleeping bags on wooden or bamboo platform beds. These strangers courteously fed them feast-like meals, and earnestly answered questions from Alfred and Ed.

The questions started out general. "How many villagers live here? Where do your children go to school?" the men would ask the tribal leaders. And eventually end with the important questions. "Have you heard about True God? Would you like someone to come to your village to tell you more about True God?"

Occasionally, a village would already have a Christian church or chapel. Then word of mouth quickly spread that a special testimony service would take place after sundown. Since most tribal villagers had never seen or touched foreign white children, Abbie, Philly and Leif always helped draw a crowd. Abbie knew the boys hated being poked by fingers as much as she did. But they tolerated it, and tried to be friendly. For they had been taught to do so for Jesus, even though they were too young and self-focused to be concerned about the souls of others as were their parents.

*   *   *

One evening of the trip turned into an unexpected experience Abbie knew she would never forget. They were about midway through the trip, and weary – not just from long days of traveling in the uncomfortable jeep, but also from visiting with strangers day after day, evening after evening.

Late in the afternoon of that particular evening, they were bumping along the dusty coastal road in the vicinity of Ta-chia. They were looking forward to the expedition's end, and not enjoying the gorgeous open view of the Pacific Ocean as much as usual.

Out of the blue, Alfred said, "Ed, why don't we stop right here and camp early tonight on the beach? It's so nice, we probably won't even need the tent."

"Well sure, why not," Ed agreed, with one of his fun winks back at the kids.

"Can we swim too?" Abbie asked, leaning forward and tapping both men excitedly.

"If the water's clean enough." Alfred grinned over his shoulder at the three of them, probably as eager to swim as they were, but more wary of what passing ships may have dumped.

He drove off the road and parked on the pebbly beach. They jumped out, their weariness forgotten. Abbie ran off to change into her swimsuit behind some bushes, while the guys changed beside the jeep.

Soon they were gliding and diving around like the mystical Yangtze River dolphins in that beautiful, turquoise-green stretch of ocean! The water cooled and cleansed their sweaty bodies. The waves were just right for body surfing. The place was surprisingly isolated, so no crowd gathered to gawk at them. They swam until sunset, each unwilling to give up the idyllic moment until absolutely necessary.

The beach was perfect for a hidden bonfire in a cave of boulders. While Philly and Leif collected driftwood, Abbie helped her father and Ed prepare a cold supper and set out their sleeping gear. Before long, they were stretched out in their sleeping bags beside the fire, gazing up at the wondrous, star-decorated sky.

"Can you hear the waves?" Abbie sleepily asked the boys. "They're calling us to come back. . . come back. . . *hui lai*. . . *hui lai*. . ."

But neither Philly nor Leif answered.

Abbie soon fell asleep, too, listening to the dads talking. Both were fluent in Mandarin, Swedish, and English, and they'd been good friends since their childhoods in China. The mix of languages they spoke that night sounded to Abbie like a musical bedtime story that slowly faded away. The last words she heard were "Noah's Ark. . . ."

* * *

Finally they reached the mountain area where Alfred and Ed first heard about the tribal ancestors' ancient boat. Nor was it easy for them to get there. Most tribesmen wouldn't even discuss the matter with Alfred and Ed. Those who did, were reluctant to reveal what they considered was a sacred and therefore secret place of their ancestors.

The ones who responded were older tribesmen, their faces and bodies blackened by multiple tattoos, signifying they had been headhunters. To Abbie, they looked fierce, but not frightening. She had visited them many times with her father when she was young and they lived in Hwalien. All five of them were intrigued by meals served in bamboo tubes filled with glutinous rice and tasty bits of meat and vegetables. And the boys said they envied the tribal people's camp-out lifestyle.

"You can't even imagine the hardships of living like this," Alfred said to the two boys. "The way they're living may look as fun as camping, but it's not. Just think of living this way every day all year long, even in the cold months and when there's not enough food for everyone, and you have to choose who gets to eat."

For several days, they enjoyed camping at the base of the mountain sacred to the tribal people. To their great disappointment, they could get no one to guide them up through the dense jungle to its summit.

Tribesmen, briefly tempted by Alfred's offers of money, eventually shook their heads "no." It was far too risky, they said. Yes, they knew men who had climbed the mountain, but no one in recent memory had returned. Were their bodies found? No, never, so the spirits were waiting to catch the next climbers. Yes, of course they knew about their ancestors' ancient boat up there, but the last people to tell about seeing it had died long before they themselves or their parents were born.

*   *   *

During the last days of their round-island trip, Noah's Ark was all the five of them talked about. They were extremely disappointed not to have reached the goal of their search. But they were also thrillingly tantalized by how close they had come, especially Abbie, who would soon be leaving for the U.S.

Alfred nodded when she said thoughtfully,

"Dad, it's almost like we were following God's footprints through the mountains, isn't it? That place really did feel sacred. Maybe in five years after Philly and Leif graduate from Morrison, the four of you will try again. If I can, I'll come back and go with you."

"Abbie" reluctantly leaves her family and Formosa, and heads to the States for college in 1959.

* * *

Abbie's Journal
Sep 19, 2007

. . . *I've just read* **In Search of Noah's Ark,** *a fascinating book printed a number of years ago about the remains of the "true" Noah's Ark that are located in a glacier in Turkey. The author's quite convincing about how these remains have been sighted and documented for more than 2000 years, as well as in other places around the world. I've inherited Dad's interest in the mystery of the ark's remains, and remember Dad showing me years ago how the Chinese character for "boat" depicts a boat-like symbol combined with the symbols for eight and people, just like in Genesis. . .*

. . .*he also showed me other characters with what seem to be embedded Judaic-Christian symbols. I don't know characters, but I know scholars have long studied and debated these connections. Dad always thought the connections might also be clues to the mysterious Stone Ten Keepers who have intrigued my family for more than a century, starting with Gramma Lizzie and her interest in the Nestorian Monument, which started our family's interest in it. I'm still thrilled Dan took my photo taken beside it this past summer in Xian. . .*

Chapter 18

Abbie's Journal
Oct 4, 2007
. . . I'm reading my second book by William E. Barrett. The first was The Left Hand of God *(1951) a compelling novel about mission work in China. Surprisingly, the protagonist was a man accidentally impersonating a Catholic priest for a time. In spite of that, he was used by God and accomplished many wonderful miracles. That book led me to this second book,* The Red Lacquered Gate *(1967), Barrett's biography of Edward Galvin, one of the founders of the Irish Columban Foreign Mission Society of priests and nuns, founded in 1916 to send Irish missioner priests to China. It reads like a captivating novel. While Father Galvin didn't keep a journal, he wrote thousands of descriptive letters, and Barrett includes quotes from many of them in the biography. Here are a few unforgettable ones:*
. . . page 275 – "I never knew what 'nothing' meant until I came to China. Poverty is hard, but hunger is terrible. And the Communists! My God, what demons they are. Robbing and killing, right and left. It is a hard country. Every single one of our missions has been attacked and looted. No one has escaped."
. . . page 272 – "God help us, we are in a fearful plight these past few weeks. . . . The Yangtze is 53 feet higher than its normal level and is rising. The distress on all sides is appalling; thousands of persons drowned, thousands dying from starvation, millions homeless. It is heartbreaking to go out, to witness these harrowing sights, to feel you are

powerless to relieve the suffering. As an added horror, there were bandits in boats – in many cases, large parties of bandits in big boats – who cruised over the vast flooded sea-like river, robbing the poor people who clung with a few rescued possessions to housetops or bits of high land. The callous brutality of these bandits was difficult to credit. They rescued no one, provided no help in an extreme situation, robbed indiscriminately and were utterly indifferent to the value of human life."

. . . yes, so tragic! I've heard similar accounts from my family and Chinese friends. So so sad. . .

Shanghai, China, 1959
Year of Swine

"Listen well, stupid old woman," the Judiciary of the People's Republic of China sternly ordered the frail, trembling woman bowed before him. "For refusing to renounce the folly of your Western education, and for spending your life uselessly painting river scenes, you now forfeit your remaining days. For the good of this Great Country, tomorrow you will be executed."

He commanded the guards, "Return this traitor to her cell. Do not waste any more rice or tea on her."

They can destroy my body, Lin Hui-ching groaned, crumpling painfully onto the fetid floor of her cell, *but they cannot destroy my soul or my art – China's art. Thanks be to True God that even here in my brutally chaotic motherland, some of my scrolls are secreted away, awaiting a new era of freedom.*

Throughout the night, thinking about her landscape scrolls with secret, microscopic Bible verses hidden on them, brought peace to her heart. Her swollen, scabbed and pustulous lips moved from time to time as she remembered the places where her scrolls hung in freedom and safety – places like Iowa, in America, where she had visited special friends decades ago. A trip of a lifetime, truly! Most amazing to her in that beautiful land of Mei-kuo was the freedom the people enjoyed, the freedom that most of them seem to take for granted. *Maybe China will have that freedom someday. Maybe the story my life and death will, in time, help win freedom here for my countrymen.*

And she remembered with deep fondness her family and friends and art-scroll apprentices. Thinking about them warmed her heart and made her forget her misery and coming death. She remembered her sister who had drowned herself so long ago in the upper Yangtze, and how she herself had restored honor to her family by taking as her artist's name characters that referred to her sister and her own wonderful foreign benefactor.

Yes, she could still remember and smile about that first trip down the Great Long River in the Gospel Boat with the then frightening-to-her missionaries named Nieh. Whatever would she have done in those days without her reassuring older cousin and her cousin's husband, Chu Boatman. *Ai yah!* Those two dear ones were long dead.

Hui-ching was grateful the Chus had not lived to suffer under China's Red regime. But what about their children and grandchildren, she wondered? Were Ta-mei and her family and the others still surviving back home in Fengshan far up the River? The last news she had heard was that one of the Chu's adopted sons who had been with the Niehs' son for years had returned home and was living in the Niehs' Great House. But that was long ago. Maybe their lives had already been taken like hers soon would be.

Wearily and painfully, she wanted to move her cramped body to a more comfortable position. But the excruciating pain of moving made her cry, so she remained in her crumpled position. As her body numbed, her thoughts moved back to the best day in her life, the day she dared say, "Yes, I believe! Because of your faithful witness and the witness of others, how can I not believe? " She was so glad she had said those words to Nieh Husband, Alfred's father, and that she had visited him in Iowa. For he had died the year after her trip to America.

In America, she had dared speak openly about being a Christian, but not when she returned to China. There she had joined the secret Stone Ten Keepers. What a miracle to find them, she thought. And she had not given away their secret, not even during the recent weeks of torture and interrogation. *Thank you, thank you, thank you, my beloved True God, for keeping my mouth silent and protecting my friends and your followers. Please, please, please grant me the courage and voice to say the name of Yeh-su out loud for the first time in my motherland before my death tomorrow. Let me be a Stephen and a Peter before I die. Ah-men! Ah-men! Ah-men!*

In the morning, Hui-ching was dragged to an execution site on the banks of the Great Long Yangtze River. Scarcely aware of those around her, in a weak voice she offered her final thanks on earth to True God of Heaven.

Then suddenly, startling everyone, she cried out

in loud voice, "Believe in Jesus and go to heaven! Believe in Jesus and go to heaven! Ah-men!

Twenty gun blasts – and ten bodies, spurting blood and body tissue, jerked into the River.

For a few minutes, the squadron of young Red Guards stared at the bodies swirling away in the murky waters now tinged reddish. A few of the guards vomited, while a few others spit with distain into the river. But several others blinked back tears. Perhaps because they had heard the old woman's words and remembered their grandmothers.

Then in careless formation with their guns on their shoulders, they marched back into the city shouting slogans of Chairman Mao, China's "great liberator and reformer."

*   *   *

Abbie's Journal
Dec 31, 2007

. . . in my nightmare last night, I was with family or friends that I knew well. We were looking through a circular moon-gate opening at a beautiful view of mountains, ocean and sky. I sensed we were someplace in Taiwan, but I couldn't place where. Suddenly, I heard or just knew that a wild animal was prowling beyond the gate, threatening our lives. We looked in panic for a place of refuge because the opening couldn't be closed. Just in time, someone pulled me through a hidden door, and we somehow held it tight against a fierce dragon-like beast.

. . . but soon we heard the beast killing whoever was left on the other side of the door keeping us safe. We couldn't save whoever it was because if we tried, the dragon would also kill us. . . what a choice! Then I awoke. . . feeling frightened and horrible for not saving someone from a terrifying death, but

so relieved it was just a dream. The meaning? Perhaps a reminder of EVIL that goes about like a roaring beast, seeking those IT can devour (I Peter 5:8), and that as a Christian, I must do more to help those I know to the safe side of the door that is sometimes hidden – just like my family has tried to do for more than a century in China, the Great Land of the Great Dragon River and the Great Dragon Wall . . .

*   *   *

"A little Taiwan maiden gleans rice in the 1950s."

GLEANERS

A little Taiwan maiden,
    In rice fields gleans today;
She gleans in fair Formosa,
    As Ruth so far away.

But she has other duties,
    Which I will tell to you:
She is her brother's keeper,
    And to her trust is true.

The best new baby buggy
    Would surely worthless be,
For no wheeled carriage here is used,
    In rice fields, all agree.

So on her back she carries
    Her sleepy brother still,
While gleaning rice for supper,
    That all may eat their fill.

But little maiden humble,
    You too must know the Way,
The Truth, the Life is Jesus,
    Who died mankind to save.

Yes, harvest fields are plentious
    And lab'rers far too few;
Will you then pray and give, friend,
    And tell the Gospel true.

A. Fred Nelson

"Alfred Newquist"

Epilog

Centuries ago as the Tang Dynasty was ending, an ancient scroll was anonymously inscribed with these Chinese characters, then secreted in an isolated monastery hidden in the shadows of the Great Wall:

When I, an aged and nameless Buddhist monk, opened the courtyard gate late yesterday afternoon, a woman stood before me whose face and body were masked by heavy cloth, and whose feet were as large as a man's. In one hand, she held more imperial gold pieces than I have seen in a long time. With the other, she directed a sword at my heart. I quickly led her to a private area. There in a low voice, harsh and trance-like, she narrated this extraordinary occurrence for me to record.

It happened, she said, on a night with no moonlight or starlight – a black night, one to beware of wandering spirit-ghosts. She paused when a serving boy brought us tea, which she sipped briefly beneath her face covering.

Continuing her account, she explained how she was the woman the others had chosen to hide and watch

and make this secret report of what she witnessed. She had hidden where her husband instructed her to, far outside the safety of their city's wall, but still many li from the Great Wall. The terrain was rocky, with scattered bushes and trees, but no dwellings or people. In a nearby valley, but one several days' walk from the monastery here, she knew with sorrow that jagged ruins still smoldered. The ruins were the remains of her people's temple destroyed by order of China's new imperial dynasty.

The woman told me she was weary and stiff by the time a column of men staggered into view. They were bent over, their faces nearly touching the earth as they pulled and heaved what she soon realized was her people's holy stone. The men were disguised as imperial executioners, and not one of them did she recognize. So she did not know if her husband was one of them, nor has she seen him since to ask him. She knows that secrets sometimes save lives

The men stopped near her hiding place, gasping for breath as they rubbed rags over their sweating bodies. Then with frenzied motions they took turns digging a deep pit several times larger than a burial cave. While most of the men dug, a few stood guard or paced around, peering into the darkness with their swords drawn. She thought she heard footsteps and whispers from the blackness beyond the pit, but she saw no one, nor did she know what to expect since had she not been told the full plan so she could not reveal it in case she was captured.

When the pit was finished, the men knelt awkwardly beside the holy stone. The woman praised their courage to me for doing what the emperor had forbidden and threatened with death by a thousand sword cuts. She counted twelve kneeling men.

Rising from their brief obeisance, with great effort and muffled groans, the men lowered the stone that was twice the height of a man into the pit. As they did so, she could faintly see its engraved symbols and characters, once reverenced, but now disgraced by imperial decree, slide from view.

With amazing speed, the men refilled the pit with earth, and planted a partially grown tree on the spot. They stomped down the surface before covering the area with rocks and twigs. While she was admiring how cleverly the task had been completed, suddenly one of the men rushed to her hiding place and thrust a bundle into her hands. Do as you will be instructed tomorrow, he whispered, bowing and stepping backwards away from her. A moment later, he and the other men disappeared into the darkness. In fear and awe, she fell to her knees. She could not remember what happened during the next hours until she found herself entering her home, wondering where to hide the dangerous bundle in her arms.

That is all you need to write, were the woman's final words to me. We sat in silence while she sipped more tea, and my brush strokes dried. When I handed her the scroll, rolled and tied, she rose and bowed as she slid it up her sleeve. I escorted her to the gate.

She knows I will keep her secret, for I do not want to risk losing my nirvana I hope is coming soon. Ai-yah! Indeed I will keep her secret. But I also feel compelled to make this second scroll, and that she does not know. Even though I do not understand the significance of what I have recorded here, my heart is confident someone will someday find this scroll who understands. And to them, may fate grant ten thousand fragrant moments of peace!

Author's Notes

Meggie's Letters:
Meggie's letters are a special tribute to my beloved Mom, Blanche Lucretia Ivers Nelson (Meggie in my China novels). Mom wrote many published articles, and always planned to write a book about the real life Mother Ruth (I still have Mom's drafts). To honor her dreams, I've used her letters exactly as she wrote them years ago with only a few minor edits, including name changes to fit the novel.

Also, you may be interested to know that my younger brother Doug (Phil in my novels) and I had three older brothers who died in China, not just two. In the summer of 2007, I tried to locate the Xian (formerly Sian) Christian Cemetery and my brothers' graves, but the site is covered with buildings. My father Fred Nelson (Alfred in my novels) also tried to locate the graves with the same result in 1987. I've heard that some of the cemetery's gravestones were protectively hidden by Christians in the Xian area, but I don't know anything more about that at this time.

Photos:
The photos throughout this novel are from Fred Nelson's collection. My father took most of them. He often included himself in photos by using a tripod, or by handing his camera to someone else. Why am I including photos in my China novels? About ten years ago I read **Cane River**, Lalita Tademy's fascinating

novel based on her Louisiana family. The book included a number of her family's photos and clippings. I thought at the time, wow, what a great way to enrich and authenticate a story. I want to do that with my novels when I write them. And now I have!

Bible Convoy:
My father, Fred Nelson, and his older brother, Oscar Nelson Beckon, are the "stars" in the fascinating little book, *Bible Convoy* by Phyllis Thompson, published in 1949 by the China Inland Mission. I have permission to use quotes from it as I have in *Dragon Wall*. The only changes I made were a few names which I changed to match the novel's names. The book itself is no longer available, but "Aunt" Phyllis's 2000 book, *China: The Reluctant Exodus*, is still available, at least on Amazon.

Morrison Academy:
Morrison Academy is a very real school in Taichung, Taiwan. It began in 1952 in a little bamboo hut-like building, and was formally organized in 1953. The board of representatives from several missions named the school after Robert Morrison (the first Protestant missionary to China, who arrived there in 1807). In addition to its main enrollment of missionary kids (MKs), the school also welcomed U.S. military, embassy, and business kids. www.mca.org.tw/

Who Is Going to Heaven?
I have permission from Jim Clayton to retell his powerful Great Wall story from his book titled, *Who Is Going to Heaven?* A book that makes you think!

Chinese Astrology:

Believers in God are warned in the Holy Bible not to follow astrology, but the Holy Bible does not say astrology is false. I believe as I've been taught – we are warned so we won't let astrology take dominance in our lives instead of God.

While the Newquists (my Gramma Lizzie's family's surname which I use in my novels to honor the mother-side of families) certainly did not practice Chinese astrology, they knew it was highly important to the Chinese, and therefore information they needed to understand. That's why I've noted the year in Chinese astrology for each chapter along with the Western year.

Chinese Romanization:

For the most part, I've used the Wade Giles Romanization (spelling) for Chinese because I grew up with it, not the more recent Hanyu Pinyin decreed by the People's Republic of China. Sometimes in the journals, because they're contemporary, I've used the Pinyin.

Peter Hessler's China Books:

Peter Hessler's non-fiction trilogy is fabulous! I especially recommend the third book in the trilogy, *Country Drive: A Journey Through China*. because it so marvelously illuminates the Great Wall today and historically. Peter took driving trips along the Great Wall over a several year period. The first two books in his trilogy are *River Town* and *Oracle Bones*.

My Imprint:

In case you've wondered about the imprint on my books, it's my own. I'm independently published, and my husband Dave created my imprint. He based it on Revelation 21:11: "Light like a most precious stone. . . ."

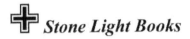 *Stone Light Books*

~ Millie Nelson Samuelson, 2012
Yesterday's Stories for Today's Inspiration

Author's Trilogy Comments

The wonderful adventure of writing historical novels began for me, the real Abbie, on the eve of this still new millennium – thanks to early retirement and a library memoir writing group.

Until then, I had never completed a story in writing, though I told many during the decades I was a busy educator and homemaker. Those were the years I lived overseas or in Kansas – and completed instead hundreds of pages of college classroom lectures, academic documents, press releases, feature articles, and oh-so many letters, emails and novel notes.

To my amazement, my memoir stories have become novels, almost like three heirloom patchwork quilts – *Hungry River* (1889 to1931), *Dragon Wall** (1933 to 1959), and *Jade Cross** (1967 to 2008). Inspired by my family's extraordinary lives in China, these story-quilts are pieced together with fictional borders. Though in truth, even the borders differ little from real life – they're just rearranged or borrowed from someone else's experience.

Some of the pieces in the story-quilts come from the journals and memoirs of my "Nilsson" grandparents who traveled up and down the Great Yangtze River during the late 1800s and early 1900s. Some pieces are from my own memory, such as our family's traumatic escape from China in 1950 down the Yangtze.

Other colorful pieces come from family letters and manuscripts – both published and unpublished.

One of these is my mother's devoted portrayal of a special missionary woman. Lovingly known as Mother Ruth (Ahlstrand), this woman gave up a life of Swedish nobility and used her inheritance to serve God beside her husband in China, where their only children are buried.

The stories I've quilted together come from a century of memories of my Anglo-American family who lived and traveled in China. Like my son who smuggled Bibles into China in the 1990s, we thought of ourselves as adventurers for God, although the Chinese often called us "foreign devils." Occasionally, however, we received the honor of being called "white Chinese" or *bai-zhong-ren*.

Centering on characters with mostly fictional names, my novels are told mainly in third person, and I'm the narrator. I chose for my aunt and myself the name disguise of Abigail and Abbie, after my favorite Old Testament character. (You can read <u>her</u> amazing story in I Samuel 25.) Most of what happens to Abbie in the novels has really happened to me. And as I am in real life to my dear Aunt Mildred, Abbie is the namesake of her Aunt Abigail, Alfred's sister and my own father Fred's real-life younger sister Mildred.

Some of my characters are scarcely disguised and not even renamed – for example, my paternal grandparents who are the main characters in **Hungry River**. I like Gramma's nickname of Lizzie from Elizabeth too much to change it. Instead of his first name Philip, I call Grampa by his last name Nils, from Nilsson in Sweden or Nelson in America. I have given them the surname of Newquist, Gramma's actual maiden name, to honor maternal surnames.

Another whose name I didn't change was that of my grandparents' first child, Hilda. At age fifteen, she was brutally killed in a 1911 uprising in Sian – martyred, my family always said. How could I change her name!

My father was the seventh of nine Nelson children. In addition to Hilda, two brothers died as babies in China. Like most of his siblings, Dad was born in China and the one perhaps most often identified as white Chinese. Dad's Swedish-American name was Albin Fridolf Nelson. In time, he changed it legally to A. Fred Nelson. His Chinese name was always *Nieh Fu De*. In my novels, the character Dad inspires is Alfred Newquist, and his character blends traits and experiences from his real brother Oscar. His other brothers – Theodore, Arthur and Edward – inspire the characters of Oliver and Johann. Alfred and his granddaughter Jeanne, who is Abbie's daughter, are both intrigued by their Swedish roots, as is my own daughter Marla Jean.

I use other slight name disguises as well. For example, my maternal grandmother was Cynthia Nettie (Clark) Ivers. In life, she was called Nettie – in my stories, Cynthia McIvers. Her daughter, my mother, was Blanche Lucretia (Ivers) Nelson. I renamed her Omega or Meggie for *alpha and omega* symbolism. Alfred and Meggie are two of the main characters in Book Two, **Dragon Wall**.* Abigail is a third improtant character. She is Nils and Lizzie's youngest child and Alfred's sister. All three are introduced in **Hungry River**.

I've also not changed the name of some our close family friends and mission associates, like Edvard Torjesen. His family's story in China is a powerful and miraculous one. Check out Ed's son Finn, and his work with Evergreen Friendship Family Service in the same area where his missionary grandfather Peter was killed by a Japanese bomb in 1939. Yes! God's marvelous over-rulings of mankind's errors are forever inspiring.

Some of my story people are combinations from real life – such as my three older brothers who died in China during wartime conditions around 1940. In the retelling, Abbie has two older brothers who died, similar to my surviving brother and me. My younger brother Doug inspires the novel character named Philip – in memory of our Grampa Philip and our brothers Philip, Daniel and Donald who were buried in China.

In addition to combining my uncles and brothers, I also combine my sons Peter and Rodney into Abbie's one son. His name is Marlan, a combination of my sons' middle names Mark and Allan. In real life, their father and my husband is David Samuelson. Of course in the Bible story, King David became the original Abigail's husband and so would be a fitting name for my character's husband. However, I rename him Daniel Samson – two more name disguises provided by unforgettable Biblical characters. He and Abbie are introduced as a couple in **Hungry River**, and featured in **Dragon Wall** and **Jade Cross**.* And Abbie is definitely the author, me.

Just as my Anglo characters are named for special people and reasons, so are my Chinese characters. For obvious reasons, I think, you need to ask me about them in private.

Besides characters' names, I have also chosen place names with purpose and care. Most are real places – with two main exceptions. Fengshan along the Great Long River is not a real place (at least according to my research). However, as I've imagined it, Fengshan is very like places my parents and grandparents lived in China. The name means Wind Mountain, and is the name of a town in Taiwan where my family once lived. Interestingly, the street address in America where I wrote about Fengshan is Windridge Drive. . . wind ridge, wind mountain. Hmm. . . I didn't notice the connection until long after I'd chosen the name Fengshan and my first novel was mostly written.

For many decades, I was deprived of even visiting my birthland because of the Communists. In 1950 when my family fled from China to Taiwan, we left behind our home and friends, as well as the graves of relatives and close friends. My family and I still feel that separation sorrow. So even though several places in America are dear to my heart, I'm never sure how to answer the question, "Where are you from?"

I have combined the places in America dear to my heart into my novel's Windridge, Indiana. Like Fengshan in China, Windridge is reminiscent of the wonderful places my family has lived in America – especially the towns of Boone, Mt. Carmel, Rockford, Janesville, McPherson, and Chesterton.

The people and places in my story-quilts are real – or in some instances, close representations. So I make no similarity coincidence disclaimer. I just hope my loved ones enjoy recognizing themselves and the places they've lived, while remembering that individual perceptions may differ (especially from a long-distance view), and that occasionally my novels are truly fiction.

Fashioning a trilogy of heirloom story-quilt novels has been personally rewarding beyond all expectations! As I examined my family's records and mementoes long stored in my China boxes, I was deeply touched by the meaningful pattern in story that emerged from the memories – memories daring, tragic, and joyous.

But most importantly, my family's stories affirm the blessings of faith in God through Jesus Christ – a faith available to every person, in every country, of every millennium!

> ~ *Millie Nelson Samuelson*
> *2012, Lunar Year of Dragon*

* ***Jade Cross*** is partially written, but only God knows when it will be published, but I hope and plan by 2014.

Newquist Family Timeline for *Hungry River* and *Dragon Wall*

1864 – Nils William Newquist is born in Sweden.

1869 – Elizabeth/Lizzie Abigail Beckman is born in Sweden.

1873 – Lizzie's family emigrates and settles in Iowa.

* * *

1889 – ***Hungry River*** begins.

1891 – Lizzie arrives in Shanghai with Bertil and Ruth Carlson, early scouts for the Salvation Army.

1892 – Nils arrives in Shanghai, working as a crewman with the *Sverige Ericsson* merchant ship.

1895 – Nils and Lizzie marry in September in Shanghai; Nils becomes an American citizen.

1896 – Nils and Lizzie travel to Fengshan for the first time with Wang Sister and Chu Boatman.

1897 – Hilda Cecilia Newquist is born in Shanghai.

1900 – Twins Alfred Nils and Adolph Nils Newquist are born in Fengshan.

1900 – Baby Adolph dies as the Newquists escape from the Boxers down the Yangtze.

1900 – The Newquists flee China and arrive in Des Moines, Iowa.

1901 – Oscar Charles Newquist is born in Des Moines, Iowa.

1903 – Nils and Charlie Beckman travel to Sweden.

1904 – Oliver Nils Newquist is born in April in Des Moines.

1904 – Nils, Charlie, and Ruth Carlson return from Sweden to Des Moines.

1904 – Nils, Lizzie, their children and Ruth return to Shanghai.

1905 – They all move to Fengshan.

1905 – Johann Adolph is born in Fengshan.

1907 – Great House is finished and they move in.

1909 – Hilda goes to Sian to boarding school for the first time.

1911 – Alfred and Oscar go to Sian to boarding school for the first time; Hilda, Oscar and other children and teachers in the school die at the hands of rebels, and are buried in the Sian Christian cemetery; Lizzie, Alfred, Oliver and Johann flee to Sweden with Ruth, while Nils remains in China.

1912 – Abigail Hilda is born in Sweden.

1913 – Lizzie and her children travel to Iowa with Ruth.

1914 – Nils reunites with Lizzie and their children in Iowa.

1915 – Nils, Lizzie, Johann, and Abigail return to China along with Ruth, while Alfred and Oliver remain with "Uncle" Oliver Bergstrom in Iowa.

1922 – Johann returns to America to live with "Uncle" Oliver Bergstrom and finish high school; Abigail goes to Sian to boarding school for the first time.

1926 – Alfred returns to China alone to work with his parents.

1929 – Abigail goes to America to attend college.

1931 – Alfred returns to America and marries Meggie (Omega McIvers); Lizzie dies unexpectedly in Fengshan, and Nils buries her in Sian beside Hilda and Oscar; the Stone Keepers are still a mystery; *Hungry River* ends.

*   *   *

1933 – **Dragon Wall** begins; Nils retires, and Alfred and Meggie take his place in China; their first son Donald Alfred is born in Shanghai; Meggie meets the family's close friend Lin Hui-ching.

1934 – Alfred, Meggie, and Donny join "Mother" Ruth Bergstrom in Sian; Meggie learns about the Nestorian Monument and the mysterious Stone Ten Keepers.

1935 – Kilby Alfred is born in Sian; Japan's aggression in China escalates.

1937 – Alfred, Meggie, their young sons, and Mother Ruth go on a donkey cart convoy, following the Great Wall in search of the Stone Keepers.

1938 – Kilby dies in the Sian area.

1941 – Alfred's sister Abigail nurses Gladys Aylward back to health.

1942 – Japan bombs Sian; Abigail/Abbie Marie is born in Sian; Donny dies in Sian; Alfred's sister Abigail and Nathan Jenson marry near Sian.

1946 – Philip Alfred is born in America.

1948 – Alfred is discharged from the Marine Corps; he and others form a motorized vehicle convoy to transport thousands of Bibles from Shanghai to Sian; Meggie, Abbie and Philly return to China; China's civil war escalates.

1950 – Alfred, Meggie and their two surviving children, Abbie and Philly, flee China to Hong Kong.

1951 – The Alfred Newquist family begins a new life, free from war for the first time in decades, on the island of Formosa; Hwalien, where the Newquists live, is severely damaged by an earthquake.

1956 – The Newquists settle in Taichung after a year in America.

1959 – Abbie graduates from Morrison; Alfred, Abbie, Philly, Ed Johnson and his son Leif travel by jeep around Formosa in search of an ancient tribal legend; Abbie reluctantly leaves Formosa for college in America; in Communist China, Lin Hui-ching is executed by Red Guards; *Dragon Wall* ends.

The Newquist family's story will continue in Book Three, *Jade Cross*, to be released by 2014, GW.

An Interview with Author Millie

An interview by agent Diana Flegal for Hartline Literary Agency's Blog on 10-13-09 with a few updates:

Millie, tell us a little bit about yourself and your writing journey that led you to self publish your books, and why you chose this non-traditional way of getting your words in print.

The seeds for my first book, *Women of the Last Supper: "We Were There Too,"* were planted decades ago in China, where I was born and raised during devastating war times. Yes, my younger brother and I are war survivors, but our three older brothers were buried in Xian.

Until seventh grade, my sporadic schooling was mostly by my missionary parents as we fled from place to place, seeking safety from bombs and anti-*foreign-devil* mobs. So during my elementary years, Dad's pocket New Testament was often my only textbook.

I still vividly remember one day reading a lesson in the Gospels, then asking, "Daddy, why didn't Jesus have any girl disciples?"

Dad looked at me with surprise and answered, "But of course, Jesus had girl disciples!" And he showed me some of the passages about the women who followed Jesus, and about the girl he brought back to life.

After my family escaped to Taiwan in 1951, we were able to subscribe to the *Reader's Digest*. What a happy day when each new issue arrived (usually months late)! It became one of my favorite textbooks. One issue had an article about Leonardo da Vinci and his famous Milan mural depicting the Last Supper. As soon as I read it, I rushed to Dad. "Look," I said, "why aren't any of Jesus' girl disciples there?"

Dad patiently explained to me that it was a very old painting, and that for some reason the painter had left out the women and the girls who would have been there because it was Passover. After all, the Last Supper was a Jewish family Seder meal. Dad didn't mention years of church tradition and theology and misinterpretation. I learned all that later.

For decades, I enjoyed researching this topic, including at the Vatican and the Louvre, where there are huge ancient paintings showing women, children, and others present at occasions similar to the Last Supper (Seder meals are like our Thanksgiving dinners). Then when I moved to Chesterton eleven years ago, for the first time I had a pastor willing to portray women at the Last Supper along with the twelve men disciples. After I wrote Lenten monologs for the twelve men disciples at my pastor's request, with only a slight hesitation he agreed to twelve women monologs as well. They created quite a stir!

People soon were asking for copies of the women monolog stories. At first, my Joy Circle at church made copy machine booklets and sold them to raise money for missions. When my son Peter saw the booklets, he urged me instead to independently publish professional books using an inexpensive online-accessed printer. So my first book was also a surprise book, especially when study groups asked me to include questions and resources. My initial, timid print run of 250 books by the online printer instantpublisher.com was gone in two weeks. Now several years later, I've sold more than 3000, mostly locally. Plus I've sold more than 1000 of my other two books. I thank God for blessing my retirement hobby!

Where did you get your inspiration for your book titled, Hungry River and its sequels in your Yangtze Dragon trilogy?

For much of my life, writing a novel was one of my dreams, partly because novels are my favorite reads, but also because I love to tell stories. I just didn't make novel-writing a priority until I moved to Chesterton at age 56. At that point, I was no longer a full-time mother and professor and academic writer. I had time and energy to work on fulfilling my novel dream! So I joined a library writing group and started attending writers conferences.

In the writing group, we wrote memoir stories. In 2000, I took a couple of these with me to the Write to

Publish conference for evaluation. Three separate staff individuals suggested I use my family's China stories in novels. I sure hadn't planned on that. My dream was always to write the great American novel, not a novel using tumultuous China, even though it was my motherland. But I took it as a sign from God, and today have written what has turned out to be a trilogy.

How did you research for your novels?

Starting with my Nelson grandparents, my family has been closely associated with China and Taiwan for over a century, so our experiences are an important part of my research. I have what I call my China boxes. They are filled with memoirs, letters, photos, articles, scrapbooks, and artifacts dating back to 1892 when my Swedish-born grandparents first went to China as single missionaries. They romanced there and were married in Shanghai in 1895. My grandfather was a prolific writer, both in Swedish and Chinese. Fortunately, when my father retired from missionary service and settled in the U.S., he translated most of his father's writings into English, for Dad was equally fluent in those two languages as well as in English. I also have stacks of writings and photos from my parents and other relatives, and my own observations, of course.

I'm an avid reader, so my research also includes hundreds of books and other resources about China, as well as recent trips to China and discussions with Chinese people. Some of my favorite authors are

Pearl Buck, Lin Yutang, Han Suyin, Lisa See, Amy Tan, Gus Lee, Jonathan D. Spence, David Aikman, Jung Chang, and Lisa Huang Fleischman.

What has been the hardest part of writing your novels and how have you overcome it?

I guess the hardest part has been securing a publisher. I sometimes wonder if I'll consider my writing completed until a traditional publishing house owns it. Although more than half a dozen publishers have been close to contracting my books, either they backed out or I did. That's why I've gone ahead and independently published *Hungry River: A Yangtze Novel* and now also *Dragon Wall: A Great Wall Novel*, along with my Last Supper book. When I speak about China and women at the Last Supper, audiences want to buy my books for themselves or for gifts. So it's been exciting to have my stories in print, and now also on Amazon's Kindle.

What do you hope people will take away from reading your novels?

That's interesting to ponder! I often pray God will speak to each reader in a personal and encouraging way through the novelized stories inspired by my family's true stories. Based on the steady, affirming feedback I receive (often email from people I don't know), God is answering that prayer.

You have two other titles that you also independently published. Tell us how they came to be.

I've already mentioned *Women of the Last Supper*. I also published a sequel to it, *Men and Women of the Last Supper: "We Were There Together."* I've sold several thousand copies of those, and now have a new version out that combines the two books. You can read about them on my website: **www.milliesbooks.org**.

What is the best writing advice you ever got? The worst?

Fortunately, I can't think of any "worst" advice. Everything has been helpful or at least interesting. The "best" advice I received is practically a cliché – "Write what you know." For me, writing about my family's traumatic century of experiences in China, especially the wars, became a healing I didn't expect. It was an area of my life I rarely talked about, but I often had terrible war nightmares. (Just ask my husband who had to awaken me many times.) I rarely have those nightmares anymore. Thank you, God!

How are you using state-of-the-art technology in your everyday writing life?

I'm old enough to remember writing on the old typewriter, and having to retype whole pages for a few changes – groan! So I still feel joy every time I sit down at my computer to write. I revel in how easy and fun it is to edit! And how easy it is to send manuscripts back and forth online. In fact, I can hardly write longhand any more. I just do occasional notes that way. For me, today's technology makes thinking and writing an adventure, and totally does away with writer's block.

Is there an area in your writing that you are working on developing more?

I grew up reading and writing when the omniscient voice or point of view was popular. Since that's now generally out of favor, it's a POV I have to be alert not to slip into, at least not too often. Sometimes I go ahead and write in it, and then come back and edit the scene into one of the character's voices. And sometimes I even leave it in. My favorite point of view to write is first person. That's why I enjoy memoir writing, and why I said "yes" to writing disciple monologs at church. It's also why the chapters in my China novels are bookended with journal entries by Abbie, who is very much me, and to give the impression she's the narrator.

What is your all-time favorite writing 'How To' book? One that you would like to recommend to other authors.

Novel writing really IS a special art and craft. So I have dozens of books about that in my collection. Years ago, I bought a copy of Penelope J. Stokes' *Writing & Selling the Christian Novel* when it was still in bound manuscript form. As soon as it came out in paperback (Writer's Digest Books), I bought another copy. I consider it my first and most important novel-writing guide. But keep in mind, I taught reading and writing about novels for years. So I'm sure I learned something from that too. I just wish I could easily put into practice everything I've learned and never have any slip-ups. Ha!

Have you had to overcome any obstacles in your writing journey?

Sure! Many! I wonder, is there a writer who hasn't had any? But I'm a firm believer in Romans 8:28, so I believe every obstacle has somehow been for my good or my writing's good or my reader's good or God's Kingdom good. *Thanks, God!*

Jade Cross
An Excerpt
Chapter One

A Yangzi River Town, China, 2008
Year of Boar

Far up the Great River in an ancient town on its banks, a mysterious relic had been lacquered and treated centuries ago to look like worthless wood. At some point in time, old cloths and straw rope were wrapped around it for further disguise.

The sacred relic was the secret possession of the Chen family – a secret passed down from mother to daughter, generation after generation, since the tenth century. Chen family members – both female and male – had died guarding the secret. But these days, no one even whispered about it.

To the dismay of Chen Lee-mei, the secret itself might soon be dead. Her mother had told her the relic was a ten shape – a priceless, sacred jade ten. But to discover its secret, she needed to find the ancient scroll that explained it and why it was in her family. And time was running out.

Ai yah, thought Lee-mei. *What indeed is the meaning of the precious stone relic? And why have we protected it with our lives and hidden it for hundreds of years deep in our earthen floor?*

She shuddered as she remembered the Red Guards dragging away her mother who was clutching her and saying softly into her ear, "Lee-mei, older daughter, you are too young. Still, today you become the keeper of our family's priceless secret. Remember all I taught you. Late last night I rehid the Scroll of the Stone Ten in. . . ."

Brutally silenced by a teeth-shattering blow from a guard, her mother hadn't finished. Nor did Lee-mei ever see her again or hear what happened to her.

In the decades since then and sometimes for years at a time, she forgot about the scroll and blocked out the memory of her bleeding, unconscious mother. But now that her ancestral home and lands were soon to be covered by waters from the new dam on the River, she needed desperately to find it. For what would happen if she lost the secret of her family's ancient, sacred treasure?

Lee-mei sighed and crossed her arms tightly. *I guess it is time to tell my sister and my daughter. It is time to ask for their help in my search. Maybe tomorrow while we are working at the new town site, I can talk with them in secret.*

*   *   *

Jade Cross, Book Three, releases in 2013 or 2014, GW.

Millie Nelson Samuelson
Yesterday's Stories for Today's Inspiration
millie@milliesbooks.org

Hungry River
An Excerpt
Author's Historical Preface

*Even if you haven't read **Hungry River** yet, you should read this preface. Ask yourself a question – Who led the revolution in China that established the Republic, and in what year? Don't know? Even if you do, try this one – True or False: The developing democratic governments in Afghanistan and Iraq struggle to control warlords and bandits in their countries not unlike those that devastated China a century ago. Or how about this one – During the Boxer Rebellion of 1900, how many Chinese were massacred compared to Westerners? Unless you knew the answers, you should keep reading. . .*

It's generally acknowledged that China has the longest history of any country in existence today – more than 6000 years. And for many centuries, it was the greatest civilization. In fact, China or *Zhong Kuo* or Middle Kingdom means "central country," referring both to importance and geographical centrality.

It's also fairly well known that gunpowder, silk, tea and spices came to the West from China a long time ago. Not so well known is the fact that Chinese ships reached the Americas centuries before the Vikings, Columbus, and other Western claimants.

Nor do most of us know much about the great

literary works of ancient China. Maybe we know names like Confucius and Lao-tze, but do we know why their writings are classics or who the other great writers are? And how about the names of even a few artists or artisans from thousands of years of amazing artworks?

This lack of knowledge, and perhaps interest, is not surprising. Until the 1800s, China was essentially closed to the Western world – to those barbarians with monstrous noses, owlish eyes, ghostly complexions, and atrocious manners. There were exceptions, of course, such as the Nestorian missionaries in the ninth century and Marco Polo in the thirteenth century, along with various other intruders who were allowed to live and tell about it.

As was true for most civilizations until modern times, China was ruled by an imperial class. These emperors and empresses and their families paralleled the royal kings and queens of the West in power and wealth. Like the West, their riches were made possible by the subjugation of millions and millions of slaves and peasants.

In between the Imperials and the wretched workers were the magistrates and the warlords with their fighting men. These magistrates and warlords controlled the workers for the Imperials in return for land and other benefits – in much the same way Western nobility and church leaders were rewarded for similar services by their royalty. Also similar were the ongoing bloody battles among warlords, between emperors, and occasionally against invaders, both Eastern and Western.

In addition to centuries of ruler-inflicted

bloodshed, rebel soldiers and peasants often formed bandit packs that terrorized and plundered anyone they could, especially travelers. Historians have estimated that in any given year, tens of thousands of bandits roamed the mountains and rivers of China. For every bandit caught and gruesomely executed, it seemed two took his place.

What you have just read is certainly an oversimplification of a complicated and corrupt sovereignty system. Even though it leaves out the gracious aspects of Chinese culture, it presents an adequate enough sketch of China at the end of the 1700s – a time when the Industrial Revolution had swept through Europe, but not over to China.

Suddenly, China was vulnerable to invasion. After thousands of years, it was no longer the center of world progress. The Great Wall was a useless defense against attacks from the sea, and China's wooden junks with their cloth sails were no match for metal ships with steam engines. Nor could the bows and arrows and swords of Chinese armies defeat armies that had learned to manufacture and use gunpowder weapons.

The same countries that conquered and colonized the Americas and other parts of the world for trade, now attempted to do the same with China. The inevitable defeat of China by Great Britain in the Opium War of 1842 was a bitter blow to a great land. As a consequence, not only were the Chinese forced to open their country to "foreign devils," they were forced to accept opium – an evil that nearly destroyed the Chinese.

However, submission to the West resulted in

more than evil. Along with the traders came missionaries and others to China. They brought with them inspiring and equalizing ideals for all people, including peasants and females.

Before long, scores of Chinese were clamoring to visit the countries of these intriguing Westerners. Thousands of young men were soon attending institutions of education in the West. Those who returned to China brought back appealing concepts like democracy, and wonders in transportation like railroads. Even peasants who went to the West as laborers discovered life could be free of oppression and dire poverty.

By the end of the 1800s, all over China secret societies were forming to overthrow the Imperials and warlords. So the bloodshed of centuries continued. Only now the peasants and those in disfavor with the Imperials were suffering for a better life for themselves, not for someone in power over them.

One of the young men who studied abroad with intense longings to improve his homeland was Sun Yat-sen. His studies led him to become a surgeon of Western medicine, and also to embrace Christianity. What radical steps for someone from a traditional Chinese family!

About this time in 1889, the story of **Hungry River,** *Yangtze Dragon Trilogy Book One, begins.*

With Japan's attack on China in 1894, Dr. Sun took another radical step. He became a powerful revolutionist against the Imperial Manchus who had resisted China's becoming a modern power. Thousands of Chinese overseas and in China responded to Sun's dynamic orations and joined his patriotic Prosper China Society.

However, not all secret societies in China were against the Imperials. Some of them were against Westerners who were seen as invaders and evil doers. One of these societies was nicknamed the Boxers. When they told the aging Empress Dowager they had magical powers against foreign devils, she believed them. Through the Boxers, she thought she saw a way to free China from foreign encroachment.

In 1900, the Empress issued a proclamation ordering the Boxers to massacre all white people throughout the land. She hoped this would restore China to its lost glory. The Boxers followed her orders, and massacred hundreds of Westerners, as well as thousands of Chinese who befriended them.

The Boxer Rebellion was quelled in several months by combined troops from Western powers. This defeat also signaled the end to the Imperial stronghold over China, and opened the door even further for revolution – as well as invasion, especially from neighboring Japan.

Sun Yat-sen's revolution finally succeeded in 1911 after years of fighting and setbacks. In 1913, China became a Republic. The next year, Sun became the Republic's first president. But when he died in 1925, peace and democracy were not yet established in his beloved country. Warlords still fought, and bandits roamed the countryside. Millions of peasants still lived desperate lives. Innocent people continued to die, including missionaries and other foreigners.

After Sun's death, two of his revolutionary

leaders (both educated for a time in church-affiliated schools) fought for control of China. These two were Chiang Kai-shek and Mao Tse-tung. Before either won, the two called a truce between their armies and fought together against Japanese invaders for more than a decade.

About this time, the story of **Hungry River** *ends in 1931*, followed by the sequels* **Dragon Wall** *and* **Jade Cross**, *Books Two and Three of the Yangtze Dragon Trilogy.*

After Japan's World War II defeat in 1945, General Chiang and General Mao resumed fighting against each other. For a time, America backed Chiang in his fight to establish a free and democratic China, then withdrew its support. Mao, in his effort to establish a Communist government throughout China, was backed by Russia. And Russia did not withdraw its support.

In 1949, General Chiang was defeated enough to flee to the Island of Taiwan (still called by its better-known Portuguese name of Formosa at the time) with what survived of his army and supporters. There he established the Republic of China, today's Taiwan.

Back in Mainland China, General Mao established the Peoples Republic of China. He eventually unified China for the first time in its long history – but at a terrible, terrible price in human lives and freedoms.

Today both Taiwan and China honor Sun Yat-sen as the Father of the Republic of China. However, the two republics face unknown future political ties. For while China claims sovereignty over Taiwan, that island country maintains its independence. Taiwan has achieved democracy and prosperity; China has yet to do so – though after decades of isolation and repression under Communism, China is an increasingly open country, gaining in power and prosperity.

With its vast untapped resources and immense population, some historians predict by the next century China will once again become the central power of the world. Should that happen, we can only hope this colossal land will also become the world's center of peace and human rights. . .
~ Millie Nelson Samuelson
2005 with 2011 revisions

*Reminder: **Dragon Wall** begins in 1933.

Hungry River
Chapter 1

Abbie's Journal
Feb 17, 2000

. . . compulsive journaling must be in my genes. For years our basement storeroom has housed my family's China boxes, filled with a century's of journals and letters and such. After the folks died, I vowed to sort through them all and read everything. But I kept procrastinating. Sure I loved reminders of our extraordinary lives in China. It was the haunting memories of suffering I couldn't bear to recall. Since our wonderful visit to China last year, at last I'm sorting and reading and remembering. As the Chinese say, it's an auspicious year to do so – it's their astrological Year of Dragon. . .

Fengshan, China, 1889
Year of Ox

Beneath the sleeping village of Fengshan rushed the Great Long River, its dark waters glowing like oiled mahogany. Here and there among turbulent swirls, huge foam shapes appeared for a moment, then disappeared.

They look like ghostly temple gods, Mei-lee thought, peering down at the River as she staggered along on painful bound feet. She clutched the infant asleep in one arm and her walking stick with the other and crept on along the steep river bank.

Once past the village, the River flowed with swiftness to a bend in its course. There it briefly became a lake, encircled by shadowy mountain peaks jutting majestically upwards. Because it was night, no junks swept by, no boatmen shouted. Only stillness and moonlight kept the River company through the gorge.

Ai! If only I had been a male, I might have gone to school. Mei-lee paused to gaze and ease her gasps. *I might have learned to brush on scrolls this scene that soothes my despair.*

Soon she reached the sacred old weeping willow standing guard between the dwellings of her village and the River. She longed to sit on the smooth earth but ached from giving birth – and from her husband's beating. Instead, she leaned on her walking stick to rest beneath the tree that had been her friend since childhood.

The tree had become her confidant the day her husband first beat her, when she first displeased him by asking to spend her fifteenth birthday at her ancestral home. She leaned painfully against her friend's familiar trunk, its strength and calm soothing her.

"See," she said softly to its leafy branches, "here is my precious second baby, born this afternoon. You are happy for me and for her, are you not? *Ai!* Thank you for your *gung-shi* wishes – though we are undeserving of your congratulations, though we are but worthless females and her birth has angered my husband."

For a long time, tears dripped from her cheeks onto the tiny black head tucked between her swelling breasts.

When at last she obeyed the River's call from

beyond the tree's gnarled roots, the moon hung low among a few fading stars. Tottering on the stumps of her bound feet, she slowly made her way down the ancient stone steps to the River's edge.

"Honorable River gods," she sobbed, "I offer you my second precious daughter. Since you received my first one, my village has had only a little hunger, and few hardships at the hands of bandits and warlords. And only a few children and old ones have been dragged off by wolves. Thank you, Honorable River gods. Thank you. Tonight I ask, please favor us again."

Moaning and swaying, she waited for a response. It came quickly. In the River's spray she saw the arms of a goddess reaching out to her.

Suddenly she gasped, "*Ai yah!*" For she saw a second pair of ghostly arms rising out of the water and beckoning to her. But she was ready, was she not? She was dressed in her best blue cotton jacket and pants. Her newborn she had tenderly swaddled in a piece of flowered cloth.

Then for the first time since stealing away from her husband's home, she turned around and gazed up towards the village wall behind the tree. There in the shadows, just as she expected, was a dark, familiar shape leaning over a cane. Next to it was a similar shape, only smaller.

Holding her precious bundle before her, Mei-lee bowed low in the direction of the shapes. She waited a moment, then turned to the River and staggered forward with bent head to meet the waiting arms.

Up at the wall, Mei-lee's mother struck her

breasts in anguish as she watched her older daughter and tiny grandbaby disappear into the churning water. Groaning, she fell to her knees beside her shivering younger daughter. Soon both began to cry out and wail aloud. Before long, women from the village surrounded them, also wailing. As the two were escorted home, no one asked why they mourned. Everyone knew.

Later that morning, Mei-lee's mother and younger sister were again joined by the village women. Together they dutifully burned spirit money and incense and offered meat pastry *bao-tzes* beneath the sacred tree at the River's edge. Chanting and moaning, the women shuddered as they sought to appease the hunger of the river gods. They begged for favor for their families, and for protection from roaming evil spirits.

All that long, sorrowful day, Mei-lee's mother waited for her husband's words. But he did not speak. Nor did he go to Mei-lee's husband to apologize for his daughter's worthless womb. His evening meal of rice and stir-fried peanut greens he ate bravely in the family's front courtyard as usual. Then he cleared his throat, spit several times into his spittoon, and spoke loudly enough to be heard by the listening neighbors.

"Wife, some say we have lost face today. Why should we care? For even worse, we have lost our pretty elder daughter because of her husband's foul temper. He is the one who should feel shamed. He should have been patient with Mei-lee or returned her to us."

He gulped and coughed. "*Tai-tai*, we will miss our kind, obedient daughter – even though the gods have favored us with sons and another daughter. *Hai!* Let us never speak to that man or his family again. May demons plague them all."

Mei-lee's weeping mother urged her husband to be seated in his favorite bamboo chair, then poured them both some tea.

"Drink, Honorable Husband," she said between sobs. "Surely, your words have defended our family and pleased our ancestors. Probably our daughter's next child would have been a grandson for us. With you I curse, her husband who has caused us loss and grief. And I curse any male descendants he may have."

That night, Mei-lee's mother lay sleepless on the family's fire-heated brick and mud *kang* bed. When muffled sobs from under the quilted *pugai* by the wall broke the painful silence, she crawled out from under her husband's *pugai* and over to her younger daughter. She lay close to Hui-ching, gently stroking the young girl's cheeks and hands.

"Be comforted, Second Daughter," she whispered under her daughter's *pugai*. "What happened to Mei-lee will not happen to you, I promise. Listen carefully now. I will unbind your feet as you have been pleading. I will persuade Ba to allow you to attend one of those schools for girls run by the fearsome foreigners."

She paused to breathe deeply several times, then continued in a low shaky voice. "If you learn to read and stroke the brush with excellence, perhaps we will not need to arrange marriage for you for many years. In time, you may even find your own husband like others are doing in these days of new ideas."

235

She felt her younger daughter's trembling body slowly calm, and the soft touch of Hui-ching's hands on her cheeks and soft voice in her ear.

"In truth, Ma, in truth? *Ai!* I vow not to disappoint you or Ba. I will learn for all of us – but especially for Mei-lee. If the gods favor me, one day I vow to paint the gorge as she longed to do. Ma, I vow to live brave and restore honor to the memory of Older Sister."

*   *   *

Abbie's Journal
Feb 24, 2000

. . . this week I've been reading one of Dad's journals I've not read before. Dad cleverly disguised it for some reason, so Phil and I overlooked it when we packed up his China things. In a 1936 entry, Dad mentions an art scroll by his family's "dear artist friend," but later Dad blacked out the name. He describes the painting as a classical one of a Great Long River gorge near Fengshan, with a "lovely calligraphy inscription." He thought it was probably valuable. Makes me very curious – who was the artist Dad was protecting? And the scroll – did he get it out of China before we escaped down the River that last dreadful time? Or did he hide or destroy it? It's not a scroll I remember. Maybe a cousin has it, or maybe it's still in Dad's China boxes. There's so much more to sort. . .

Hungry River: A Yangtze Novel
available from Amazon.com (print & Kindle)
or www.milliesbooks.org

Women of the Last Supper: "We Were There Too"
An Excerpt

Study questions and dramatization suggestions
are available at *www.milliesbooks.org*.

Author Millie's Comments

*My comments here have appeared as articles in newspapers
and magazines.*

Does your church have a Last Supper painting
or banner hanging in a prominent place? Is it a
portrayal with women present – maybe serving the
meal, standing in the background, or sitting at the feet
of Jesus?

My church has a banner like that.

During Lent and Easter, does your church have
enactments of the Last Supper with women present
along with the Twelve?

Mine does.

But it wasn't always so.

* * *

The roles of women in Christianity have long
fascinated me. One of my vivid childhood memories
from China is asking, "Daddy, why didn't Jesus have
any girl disciples?"

My missionary father answered, "Why, of course he did." Then he showed me some of the Gospel passages in his pocket New Testament about the "girls" and women who followed Jesus along with the men.

I grew up during a devastating time in China, a time much like the Holy Land Jesus knew. China was in the midst of disastrous wars, including the civil war between the Communists of Mao Tse-tung and the Nationalists of Chiang Kai-shek. My family kept fleeing from place to place, losing everything we owned many times, including my school books.

Since normal schooling was impossible, Dad's worn New Testament was often my only textbook. Gospel stories are still my favorites, especially stories about girls and women. And there are more of those in the Bible than most of us realize – like the tantalizing bits of stories about the women who followed Jesus, including those who must have been present at the Last Supper.

*   *   *

Not long after my family had escaped from China and settled safely in Taiwan, I saw a picture of Leonardo da Vinci's Last Supper painting in a magazine. I rushed to Dad and said, "Look, why aren't there any girls at the Last Supper?"

He answered, "The women were there. They just aren't shown in this painting." He didn't try to explain about it being on the wall of a monastery dining hall in Milan, or centuries of church theology and tradition. Instead, Dad patiently showed me in the Gospel accounts how the women were there with Jesus and his twelve closest men disciples <u>right before</u> the Last

Supper and <u>right after</u> it.

So even though they were not named, weren't the women there with Jesus at the Last Supper together with the men? I'm sure they were!

As I have studied the Bible more deeply, I've discovered women often weren't named. But that didn't mean they weren't there – like in the genealogies (and we all know women had to be there).

During my lifetime, I've read hundreds of books and articles about women and Christianity, watched dozens of shows and movies, and been part of numerous discussions on this topic. So imagine my excitement when my husband Dave and I traveled a few years ago to the Vatican and then the Louvre, and there viewed ancient, wall-sized paintings of the Last Supper portraying women and children along with the men. Wow!

About the same time, we joined a church with a pastor and a women's group daring enough to support the biblically and culturally based concept of women present at the Last Supper. And now, our church's Last Supper enactments include twelve women, along with Christ and the Twelve.

If you could suggest twelve women disciples of Jesus likely present at the Last Supper (to parallel the twelve men disciples closest to Jesus), who would you name? Perhaps the same "twelve" I have.

And from the many, many children that Jesus connected with during his ministry, who might have celebrated his last Passover feast before his crucifixion with him? I suggest at least six in this book, referred to in the stories of Jairus's daughter and John Mark.

*   *   *

According to Gospel accounts and Christian tradition, Jesus' mother Mary was one of his most faithful followers. Over the centuries, many scholars have even called her his first disciple. So surely, she attended that last Passover, a family Seder meal, with her son.

Mary knew before his birth who her son would become, although she didn't know how. The Gospels tell us she was the one who urged him to perform his first public miracle of water to wine. How did she know he could do it? She must have seen him perform earlier miracles at home. In fact, Christian tradition includes some of those miracles.

Mary from Magdala was another Mary likely present at the Last Supper, and certainly not in the role novelized by Dan Brown in *The Da Vinci Code*. In contrast to Brown's portrayal, many scholars have suggested she was the same age as Jesus' Mother, or even older. In the context of the Gospels, that makes historical and cultural sense, a lot more sense than Brown's portrayal which is blasphemous even though he calls it "fictional."

But Brown got one thing right – he placed Mary Magdalene at the Last Supper. She <u>was</u> an important disciple.

Famous educational colleges at Oxford and Cambridge named for Mary Magdalene testify to her scholarly reputation in the early church, as do the numerous churches throughout the world named for her. Some of these churches have been in continuing existence since the first century. They witness to Mary's position in the early church, an importance nearly lost by most Western churches, but not by the Eastern churches who have always highly regarded her and not confused her with another Mary.

The Gospel writers were always careful to distinguish Mary Magdalene from the several other women named Mary who followed Jesus. But the same cannot be said for numerous Western scholars, ministers, and popes of the past two millennia. They have frequently (purposely?) confused Mary Magdalene with another, with the Mary who was an immoral woman before she met Jesus.

That Mary may well have been the sister of Martha and Lazarus of Bethany. What a wonderful transformation Jesus caused in her life! So surely she would have been at the Last Supper, sitting and listening one more time at Jesus' feet. And there's every reason to believe her sister Martha would have been there too, helping cook and serve that last Passover meal Jesus celebrated with his followers, just as she had many other meals.

Who were the other women likely there?

For one, Peter's wife. The Bible and history do not name her, but the Gospels tell us the story of Jesus healing her mother. And Paul wrote to the Corinthians that she traveled everywhere with her husband Peter. So I don't think she missed that important meal. And neither would have Salome, another of the women mentioned in the Gospels. She was the wife of Zebedee and, according to some, the sister of Jesus' mother. That means she was Jesus' aunt, and her sons James and John were his cousins.

Like Salome and her family, many of Jesus' close followers knew and admired him long before they became his disciples. Think of the stories they'll share with us someday in heaven, the stories John's Gospel tells us were so many they would fill the world.

Two more women who followed Jesus because he had healed them were Joanna and Susanna. They are mentioned several times together by name. Maybe they were twins.* From the Gospels, we know Joanna's husband was Chuza. He was King Herod's steward, so Joanna had royal and powerful connections in addition to wealth.

Four other women followers of Jesus likely present at the Last Supper were Mary, the mother of John Mark, and her servant Rhoda; Naomi,* the woman healed of a twelve-year hemorrhage; and Judith,* Joseph of Arimathea's wife. She's not mentioned in the Gospels, but Josephus Flavius, the Jewish historian, refers to her.

Interestingly, Judith was probably Jesus' great-aunt. For according to Christian tradition (especially the Glastonbury tradition), Joseph of Arimathea was Jesus' mother's uncle. There's even a good chance the Last Supper took place in their Jerusalem home. And why not, if Mary was their niece and Jesus their beloved great-nephew. However, it's even more likely the Last Supper took place in the home of Mary of Jerusalem, the mother of John Mark. That is the home I've chosen for my vignettes. Its upper room was spacious and elegant, and could easily accommodate a couple hundred people.

*   *   *

We know for sure that most of the twelve women I've described were among the women of wealth mentioned in the Gospels who traveled with Jesus and his disciples, often providing for them from their own resources. And there's a strong possibility all twelve of them were there, along with numerous children. My research convinces me they celebrated that special family Passover feast with Jesus, and provided the meal as they had countless others, including the previous two Passovers of Jesus' ministry.

So go for it! Do what my church and I have daringly done. Honor the women of the Last Supper in your paintings and other portrayals. For surely, women and children were there with Jesus and the Twelve and other men.

* * *

*Naomi, **Judith**, and **twins** are names given based on biblical and historical plausibility.*

~ Millie N.S., 2010

Chapter 1

BLESSED SISTERS:
SALOME and MARY

Salome, Aunt of Jesus

I am Salome, one of Jesus' close women followers. From this moment on, please forget that I have the same name as King Herod's unspeakable step-daughter.

Instead, remember that I was the sister of Mary, Jesus' mother, and blessed to be Jesus' aunt. So of course, I was present at the Last Supper, as were other women who were also close followers of our Lord.

Let me remind you who the women of the Last Supper were – the women whose stories follow mine, along with the men's and children's.

First was my beloved sister Mary, known for all time as the blessed Mother of Jesus. Next were Lazarus' sisters: Mary, a redeemed adulteress, and Martha, whose spacious Bethany home Jesus loved to visit.

Mary Magdalene was also there. She was a brilliant woman from whom Jesus cast out many demons, and who became known as the thirteenth apostle in the early Christian church. The unnamed wife of Peter was there, too. Many years later and after traveling with Peter on his missionary journeys, Peter's wife was crucified before him to amuse the Romans.

Mary, the mother of John Mark and in whose palatial home we celebrated the Passover feast that evening, was there with her devoted servant Rhoda. As was Naomi,* who no longer had to stay away from such celebrations because Jesus had healed her twelve-year hemorrhage and uncleanness.

The twins* Joanna and Susanna bravely came, in spite of being the wives of men who were politically prominent in King Herod's court. My Aunt Judith and Uncle Joseph Arimathea were also there in spite of their positions in the community. My uncle was a wealthy merchant and a member of the Jewish Sanhedrin Council in Jerusalem. At the time of the Last Supper, he was still a secret follower of Jesus. But that ended when he buried Jesus in his own tomb.

Now back to my story. As you may recall from

Biblical and historical records, before my marriage I was from Nazareth, located in the southern part of the province of Galilee. In Aramaic, Nazareth means "watchtower," a fitting name for my hometown. It overlooked an important road, frequented by trade caravans and Roman troops.

Because traders and soldiers often camped in our community during their travels, other Jews joked, "Can anything good come out of Nazareth?"

My nephew Jesus certainly changed that perception, didn't he?

Many families living in the Nazareth area were from the Tribe of Judah and, like my family, were descendants of the royal line of David.

Because of our royal heritage, my sister Mary and I were fortunate to have more privileges than many young women of our time. Although our own family's circumstances were reduced by misfortune, we had many caring, generous relatives. Among these were Uncle Joseph and Aunt Judith. And I'm sure you remember reading in the Gospels about our mother's cousin Elizabeth and her influential husband, the priest Zacharias.

As Mary and I were growing up, these relatives and others encouraged us to have strong faith in Yahweh. They taught us at home from the Scrolls of the Law. To them and our beloved mother Anne, we were not just girls, but girls with a special heritage and purpose.

Who knew what Yahweh might require of us? We might become another Miriam or Deborah, Esther or Ruth, or even the mother of the promised Messiah.

What Jewish young woman of my time didn't long for that wonderful possibility!

When my sister and I were old enough to marry, our mother Anne and other relatives began the search for suitable husbands for us. Because Mother wanted us to have happy marriages, the search was not a hurried one. In time, I married Zebedee, a prosperous fisherman from the Sea of Galilee. And Mary married Joseph, a well-known carpenter from our hometown of Nazareth.

When our children were growing up, playing and working together, we didn't know what the future held. But we did know Jesus was somehow special, and that whatever became of him would affect us all.

What if he really became the Messiah, the King of the Jews, as we increasingly hoped? If so, I looked forward to my sons James and John being right there beside him, serving as his closest advisers and willing to protect him to the death.

I even mentioned to Mary several times how I liked to imagine the three of them grown up and dressed in royal robes, ruling together over a peaceful and prosperous kingdom.

She would look off into the distance as she replied, "Well you know, Salome, the ways of Yahweh are often not our ways. I just hope that whatever happens, our families will always be there for each other."

Yes, Mary was right all those years ago when she quietly and repeatedly reminded me that God's ways are often not our ways. But I learned not to be afraid, that no matter what happens to those who follow Christ, God uses everything for the glory of the Kingdom.

Yes! Those of us who followed Jesus were all ordinary people transformed by the power of Jesus Christ. You, too, can experience this transformation, and live or die for the glory of God. May it be so in your life as it was in ours.

*   *   *

Mary, Mother of Jesus

I am Mary of Nazareth, the mother of Jesus. I was his most loyal follower present at the Last Supper – the sacred event Christians remember each time they celebrate Holy Communion.

Yes, I was a mother uniquely blessed, but also one acquainted with deepest grief. My soul still magnifies the Lord when I recall the extraordinary events of my life. For whoever would have thought that Yahweh would choose someone from Nazareth to bring into the world the Messiah – Jesus, our Savior and Redeemer!

Joseph's family and mine were from the Tribe of Judah. We were both descendants of the royal line of David. Had we lived before the terrible wars and captivities of the Jewish people, we would have been called Prince Joseph and Princess Mary.

Ponder that a moment – makes the title *Prince of Peace* for my son Jesus more meaningful, doesn't it? Ah yes, because of Jesus, our family life was divinely blessed, with never a dull moment. Looking back, I can see that for years he practiced telling parables and working miracles on us – and on other people and even animals.

So it's not surprising that in time, Jesus' woodworking skills surpassed even Joseph's. I remember the day he told his disciples that his *"yoke was easy."* I couldn't help smiling as I thought of the Galilean men who waited months to purchase yokes carved by Jesus. He was famous for his yokes that made burden bearing so much easier for oxen, as well as humans.

While life with Jesus was wonderful, I'd be wrong to give the impression it was stress-free. Remember the time he stayed in Jerusalem at the Holy Temple, and frightened Joseph and me so? Nor was that the last time I didn't know where he was for days or even weeks at a time. But I learned not to worry, and to commit him to God, his true Father in heaven.

Like everyone else, I wasn't sure how Jesus' divine calling to deliver his people would be manifested. I kept waiting and watching and wondering. Then one day at a wedding reception feast in Cana, I felt something within compelling me to urge Jesus to reveal his heavenly purpose.

If you aren't familiar with the story, review it in my nephew John's Gospel. The wording is somewhat puzzling, but the outcome is clear. In spite of his reluctance, Jesus' divine ministry began publicly with that miraculous water-to-wine wedding event.

From then on, the few years left to Jesus on earth passed so quickly.

As you might expect, right from the beginning of Jesus' ministry, I was his most loyal follower – and one of his first women disciples. Yes, Jesus had his band of twelve men disciples. But as the Gospels state, there were many others who were also his close disciples, including numerous women. Most of those women were my age – in other words, well past mid-life and with empty nests. A few were elderly and a few were young, not yet mothers, such as Rhoda, Mary's devoted servant.

When you read the Gospels carefully, you will note that many of us women were with Jesus <u>right before</u> his last Passover supper with the Twelve. And we were there <u>right after</u> the Last Supper, as well as throughout the dreadful events that followed. So where were we women disciples <u>during</u> the Last Supper?

Don't you suppose we were there then too, together with the men and Jesus? Don't you suppose we prepared the Passover and served it as we had served countless other meals?

Of course, we were there, as ancient paintings of the Last Supper in Europe portray so magnificently. We just weren't there in da Vinci's famous mural on the wall of the monastery dining hall in Milan – the artwork that has dominated perceptions for far too long.

On that unforgettable Passover night, in my heart I sensed Jesus would not become our Messiah in the way we had expected. He would not become a human King of the Jews. When he was put on trial for blasphemy, and then so cruelly tortured and crucified, my soul was pierced. Ah, what agony! Just as Simeon had prophesied decades before.

But I never stopped trusting. I knew Yahweh would keep His promise to me and to the entire world. And God did, through His Holy Son, who was also my beloved son – the risen Lord and Savior of all who believe.

Yes! Salome and I were just ordinary sisters transformed by the power of Jesus Christ. You, too, can experience this transformation, and live or die for the glory of God. May it be so in your life as it was in ours.

* * *

New Testament references for Chapter 1:
Salome, Mary's sister: _Matthew_ 20:20-28; _Mark_ 15:40-41, 16:1; _Luke_ 23:44-49; _John_ 19:25-27.
Mary, Jesus' Mother: _Matthew_ 2:13-18, 13:55-56; _Mark_ 6:3; _Luke_ 1, 2, 8:19-21; _John_ 2:1-12, 19:25-27; _Acts_ 1:14.

Women of the Last Supper

available from Amazon.com (print & Kindle)
or www.milliesbooks.org

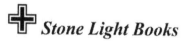 **Stone Light Books**

Yesterday's Stories for Today's Inspiration
www.MilliesBooks.org